Petra K

—— and the ——

BLACKHEARTS

A NOVEL

Petra K

—— and the ——

BLACKHEARTS

A NOVEL

M. Henderson Ellis

Young Europe Books

Young Europe Books
is an imprint of
New Europe Books

Published by New Europe Books, 2014
Williamstown, Massachusetts
www.NewEuropeBooks.com
Copyright © M. Henderson Ellis, 2014
Cover design by Hadley Kincade
Cover illustration by Laszló Hackl

ISBN: 978-0-9850623-8-5

Cataloging-in-Publication Data is available from the Library of
Congress.

Printed in the United States of America on acid-free paper.

Chapter 1

It was one of those things you were supposed to not see, or
pretend wasn't happening. A great red wolfhound chased a
small boy through the crowd, across Nerudova Square, toward the bridge. They were specks in the distance, winding their
way through the tourists and shoppers who frequented the kiosks
beneath the Imperial Palace. Not far behind, a Boot officer followed, dressed in a red and black uniform, trying to keep up with
his hound. The boy scampered between the legs of stands selling
sweet, amber-colored raisin wine, upsetting a display of crystal de-
canters, which came crashing down to the cobblestone beneath.
Even then, people turned their backs and went about their own
business. It is just what you did when the Boot was involved.

From where I stood, at the top of the square, I could see
them moving, insect-sized, the wolfhound right on the boy's heels,
as though it was a furry tail trailing behind him. Then, in an open
space, the dog caught up. He must have bit the boy's ankle, for
the boy went sprawling on the stone. The dog loomed over the
him, barking viciously. Then, from the sack that had fallen out of
the boy's grasp, a flurry of shapes emerged. It took me a moment

to realize it was a *muse* of tiny dragonka, small as hummingbirds, panicking in the open air. My heart lifted in my chest, as though it too had wings, at the sight of the dragonka in danger. The dog, also, instinctually forgot the boy, jumping toward the minute creatures, nipping at the air where they flew in dizzy circles. Then the Boot officer arrived. With a black net he produced from his holster, he began to pluck the dragonka from the air, like catching butterflies. In the confusion, the boy had time to pick his empty sack from the ground and flee again. In no time, the hound was after him, cutting through the crowd, toward Karlow Bridge, the chase continuing out of sight.

"Petra K," my teacher beckoned. It was our first field trip of the year, and Miss Kavanova did not want anything to go wrong. "Let's go already!" I had been lagging behind, and now they were all waiting on me.

"Did you see that?" I asked, looking around.

"See what, Strangeling?" called my classmate Tatiana, using her own personal nickname for me. "Was your father pickpocketing old ladies again?" Her friends snickered. It wasn't funny, but that wasn't the point. Bianka, Sonia, Lenka, Margo, and Zsofia were girls who came from the powerful families that lived beneath the Palace, daughters of poppy barons, ministers, aristocrats; families that could afford to keep show-dragonka of their own. They could laugh off whatever they wanted, including me.

"Petra K," said Miss Kavanova. "You are going to make us late."

"But I saw something," I insisted.

Miss Kavanova joined me at my side. We looked out over the square together. But by this time the boy and hound had disappeared from sight. Instead we saw shoppers browsing the black velvet portraits of champion dragonka, marionette stands entertaining tourists, and automatons selling fortunes. Business as usual.

"I *saw* something," I repeated, though I knew it was no use.

"Well I don't see anything, and neither did you, *OK?*" she said firmly, putting her hand on my shoulder, guiding me away.

Like I said, it was as if nothing had happened.

BEFORE OPENING THE DOOR to Ludmilla's Cosmetics Emporium, the Newt doorman bowed to us and kissed Miss Kavanova's hand. She reddened in embarrassment. He was dressed in black coattails, wore a bowler hat, and stood upright, no taller than any of the class, his forest-green skin oiled and shining, a wide lizardy smile spreading across his face, as though we were flies he was about to snap up. Once inside, we were greeted by gleaming marble floors, glass cases that displayed the latest products, and Persian rugs that led to departments deeper within the esteemed store.

Most of the other girls' mothers were regulars there, so they were used to the unique novelty of Ludmilla's marketing: one day there would be an oriental theme, complete with sales girls dressed in kimonos; the next day the store would be adorned with yellow-brick paths with dwarves to guide customers from room to room. Another day all the products would be cleared from the shelves but for one extremely expensive hand cream, which would be auctioned off at a dizzyingly high price. At Ludmilla's you never knew what you would get: open a dressing room door and you might find a dozen bats (which the former sorceress had bred in bright colors: mint green, carmine, and peach) bursting from the space. Look in a mirror to check a shade of eye shadow and find the reflection of yourself as you would have looked a decade earlier.

"Stay here, I will go find our guide," said Miss Kavanova.

The others waited until Miss Kavanova walked away, then formed a circle.

"Did you see her face when the doorman kissed her? She looked like she enjoyed it. I bet she has some *newt* blood in her," said Tatiana. Lenka, Sonia, Margo, and Bianka all laughed.

"I knew there was a reason she makes me squirm," I quipped, poking my head into their midst. I couldn't help it. I didn't want to be disrespectful of Miss Kavanova—but the joke seemed too obvious to pass up. Tatiana looked at me, her eyes squinting as though she was trying to determine exactly what kind of bug I was, and how best to step on me. "I don't get it," she said.

"She makes me squirm. You know, because she's a teacher. And she's a *newt*," I backtracked. I drew that last word out and arched my eyebrows in what I can only maintain was an accidental imitation of Tatiana. The class laughed, but not at me. They were laughing at my version of Tatiana. This meant certain doom. Where was Miss Kavanova? I immediately raised my sleeve to my mouth and began to gnaw anxiously. I had chewed through one sweater already this year.

"Let's go, children," commanded our teacher, returning with a small woman with tight, porcelain skin. It was Ludmilla *herself*. "And Petra K, get your sleeve out of your mouth and tuck your shirttails in. We still have a reputation to keep up while away from The Pava School." Tatiana looked at me in a way that meant we would be resolving my breech later, then she turned her attention to our host.

"Welcome to my flagship store," said Ludmilla, with a gracious wave of her arm. In a black cocktail dress, the proprietor looked the picture of old Pavain refinement. As long as she had been in business, Ludmilla, who came from a long line of renowned sorceresses, never appeared to age, though her face took on a tightness, as though her hair was pulling her skin back. There was always the smell of scented ointments about her, thus it was speculated in the Pava gossip columns that she was perpetually using herself as a guinea pig for her own cosmetics and was perhaps her own best customer. It was only when she held her left hand up that the true impact of her personality was felt: a furry spider rested in her palm and her fingers were laced with webbing, the mark of a true practitioner. I also noticed two bright red wounds on the woman's neck, cosmetic decorations that looked like she had been bitten by vampire fangs. It was the fashion at the time in Pava and most of the girls in my class had worn fang bites until the administration had declared them antisocial.

"I bet most of you have been here before, but I am quite sure none have been in the laboratories in the chambers beneath the store. To be honest, nobody outside of our own employees have. You are very lucky to have this opportunity." Tatiana elbowed Sonia, reminding her that it was her father, the district Boot commander, who had facilitated the outing. "And I'm sure you will not be disappointed."

Ludmilla led the group toward the back of the store. We filed through the doors marked "Authorized Personnel Only." Once in the back chambers, it was a world of difference from the gleaming, sparkling showroom. This was a dreary, damp chamber, with bare stone walls, and I thought I could make out shackles in the dark. Shelves of stock lined the room: a small fortune's worth of cosmetics towered above us. A group of card-playing homunculi stock boys scattered at our arrival, and tried to look busy after a punishing look from the owner. One tiny clerk scampered up a ladder on runners to gather an order, which he then harnessed to a bat to be flown back to the showroom.

"This way," said Ludmilla. We bypassed the stockroom and were taken farther still into the depths of the building. The woman applied a key from around her neck to a lock and an entire wall spun from its place, revealing the chambers that housed her laboratories. "Keep quiet, and don't touch anything," she commanded.

Once inside, we huddled together like a bouquet of flowers: all gaping mouths and wide eyes, looking about ourselves in bewilderment. There were crucibles bubbling over blue-flaming burners, rows of test tubes that masked technicians were feeding with fragrance-filled tear droppers, and the essence of flowers and herbs being distilled in large glass beakers.

"Well what did you expect," said the proprietress, "a witch's cauldron?" None of us wanted to admit it, but that is *exactly* what we expected. Ludmilla had been one of the foremost practicing sorceresses of Pava, before such practices were outlawed, and she turned her webbed hand to cosmetics. "Come, perhaps this will be more to your liking," beckoned our guide. She ushered us through the lab and to another door. Before she opened it, she passed out earphones.

"This is where we keep our pherophone laboratory," she said. "You never can be too careful." Inside, to our amazement, there was a muse of dragonka, housed in gilded cages. In front of them was a technician holding an orchestra conductor's wand.

"Shall we give our guests a little listen to the sound of our latest scent?"

"Sound," spat Tatiana. "Perfume doesn't *sound* like anything."

"That is what you think," said Ludmilla archly, before nodding to the conductor. With a tap of his wand, the dragonka sprang to attention. He lifted the wand in the air, then let it fall. With that, the dragonka raised their snouts and began to sing.

Before smelling a thing I was overcome by the hypnotic charm that was delivered along with the song, so like a tasteless poison in wine. That's what happens when a dragonka sings; it inadvertently takes the listener to another place, outside the realm of their reality. Sometimes it is a path into the listener's memory; sometimes they are transported to a dreamlike place that would be forgotten when they wake; sometimes the listener is given a window to the spirit world, or granted a vision of the future. Singing dragonka were usually muzzled, and allowed to perform only at well-orchestrated ceremonies, or in the dead of night at pagan summer festivals. Such is the power of the song that sprang from the throats of dragon offspring, which ancient Pavians had bred into the pets, owned by so many of my classmates.

Only now, the song was having another effect. It made me woozy, but at the same time, I felt myself getting lost in a strange scent. Next to the dragonka cages, I noticed a lab assistant hovering over a brass machine that was emitting colored steam. As the dragonka song changed in tempo and tone, so did the colors of stream rising from the contraption. And the smell that was coming from the colored steam was gorgeous. An odor tickled my nose that smelled like bison grass, followed by deep bassoon notes of fresh clipped heliotrope and melting candle wax.

"Just a whiff," Ludmilla cautioned the conductor, who cut the dragonka song short. "You see, the notes correspond to scents, which the pherophone translates. We collect the steam and refine it into perfume. Now follow me again, and I will show you some of the raw materials." Ludmilla led us to a smaller door that opened up on a room the size of a large closet, into which we all crowded.

From a rack she pulled various vials, each filled with a different exotic material: Bulgaryn rose petals, vanilla seeds from Madagascar, Hymilayn jasmine, Swabiland honeysuckle, plus more bizarre scents of Greater Kori tonka bean essence, mold from the wall of Francul's oldest cathedral, oil from the fur of Ruskyn minks, and refined narwhale blubber, which Ludmilla insisted was essential in the most exclusive perfumes.

"This is our newest scent," Ludmilla declared proudly, unlocking a combination safe and withdrawing a black crystal bottle. "We are still testing it, but no harm can come in giving you a sniff." With that she sprayed the bottle in the air, and at once six girls' noses rose to meet the intoxicating smell. It was like nothing I had experienced before, like breathing in atomized silk, at once oily and sweet, mixed with some ancient unrecognizable spice. I had the feeling of being back in our old house under the palace, and the luxuries we had there. Memories flooded my mind—of my mother in the garden, of my father in his black cape.

"That is lovely," cooed Miss Kavanova, snapping me out of my reverie.

"I feel strange," I said.

"How much does it cost?," asked Tatiana. "I want it."

"This is not for sale, not yet at least," replied Ludmilla, closing the perfume bottle back in the safe. I saw Tatiana's mouth tighten at the refusal, which made her look a good deal older than she was.

When the tour was over, Ludmilla gathered us at the exit.

"I hope you have all enjoyed your visit," she said. "Any questions?"

In a low mood, I wanted to ask the esteemed practitioner: "*Is it better to be alone and smart than to belong and be stupid? Do the things that make you special, also make you different, and not in a good way?*" But I kept my mouth shut—besides, I thought I already knew the answers, and they weren't hopeful.

"I have a little parting gift for each of you," Ludmilla said. Her Newt doorman circulated among us, passing out shopping bags with the elegant Ludmilla's Cosmetics logo on the side.

Before departing, the class graciously thanked their host; even Tatiana managed a curtsey.

The others waited until they were in the school garden to open their gift bags, which contained sample sizes of cosmetics. I didn't bother with mine; cosmetics held no interest for me.

"Got it," said Tatiana, throwing her hand-cream aside. "Got it," she said of the lipstick. "Got it, in super size," she said of the citrus perfume. "What a rip-off, I've already got it all. Strangeling, let me see what you have!" she said, and grabbed the bag out of my hands before I could resist. "And what is this?" she said, pulling a black crystal vial from my bag. She then held it up to the sun, as though examining a gem for flaws. It looked like the bottle Ludmilla had sampled for us.

"It was in my bag," I said. "Didn't everybody get a bottle?"

"No!" said Tatiana with a sudden rage. "Did anybody else get one?"

The others checked their bags, but I was the only one with the perfume.

"You can have it," I declared, though the other girl had already put it in her purse.

"She must have stolen it," snickered Margo.

"What are you," said Sonia, "some kind of dirty criminal?"

"Here," Tatiana said, handing me her gift bag and mumbling something about a trade, then wandering off, followed by her coterie of friends. "Come on Zsofia," she called over her shoulder. That was strange, for they had never allowed Zsofia to tag along before. She was *my* friend, which contaminated her in the eyes of the others. Zsofia looked confused: we had a plan to go in on a bag of a poppy buns together and pass the afternoon watching the dragonka being trained in the park. Zsofia looked back and forth between me and the others, gave me a pleading, pitiful look, then frowned and ran after Tatiana.

Chapter 2

In a low, sulky mood, I walked home, dragonflies buzzing around my head as I crossed the Karlow Bridge. As always, I made my way alone, because I lived in Jozseftown, which was either the city's oldest, most historical quarter, or its most degenerate ghetto, depending on whom you asked. And don't ask my classmates: their opinion has been made clear, and in this case, I have to agree with them. We used to live under the Palace, like the other girls, until my father disappeared while buying the year's stock of tea in Indya. Then we were forced to move from someplace beautiful and green to someplace colorless, a place that always smelled of boiled cabbage. To be from Jozseftown is to be branded an outcast, or at least somebody worthy of deep suspicion. Shopkeepers never tire of reciting how, through the centuries, the ghetto had been home to the city's most illustrious magicians, both authentic and fake, as well as a refuge for criminals on the run. But mostly, poor people lived there, in Jozseftown. The dark-skinned Half Nots, and the Zsida, who were prohibited from living anywhere else, commanded by custom and law to live behind the walled quarter. And people with nowhere else to go. People like me and my mother.

I walked under the arched gate that signaled the entrance to Jozseftown. Almost immediately the vibrantly colored houses turned to gray, soot-encrusted tenements, decrepit and vandalized places that appeared barely inhabitable. I wound my way through the knotty streets, past the betting galleries filled with dark-eyed Half Nots, and the Zsida-owned shops that sold antique books on mysticism or astronomical maps charting the outer depths of the galaxy. As always, vendors perked up at the sight of somebody in a Pava School uniform, at the possibility of a sale, until they realized it was just me, Petra K, one of their own. My face reddened as they turned their backs.

I stopped short at a corner on Goat Square. I lived on the other side, but dead in the center of the square was a brightly painted cart, which was being drawn by a stout pig. Two boys wearing dusty, oversized smoking jackets were chasing each other around the cart. A third was handing a vial to a man dressed in farmer's garb, and accepting a handful of kuna in return. A dark Half Not girl was corralling prospective customers from the afternoon crowd.

"Revenge potions, falling in love potions, come one come all!" cried the littlest one, who wore a top hat a few sizes too big, so it covered his whole head, with two eyes cut out to see through.

Charlatans, ripping off tourists with their fake potions. I'd been forbidden by Mother from talking to them or those of their sort. Gangs of children made homeless by the Boot, they congregated in Jozseftown, where they could live and conduct whatever shady business kept them alive, without interference from the government police and their red hounds. I always passed silently, no matter what insults they yelled my way. On this day, I did my best to slip by, keeping to the outer perimeter of the square. But the gang's smallest, vigilant to any potential customer in the vicinity, called out to me.

"Hey you!" he said, racing over, his black hat bobbing like a piston in a steam engine. I tried to ignore him, but it was too late. The others were alerted, and followed him. "What are you looking for?" he said. "Falling in love potions, revenge spells, shape-shifting ones? We got 'em all." He pulled a small vial from his pocket and opened it: a green mist rose from its mouth. "The real thing."

"I'm fine," I said.

"I bet you need one to grow taller," he said, a bit snidely.

"Who's talking?" I retorted. It was a bad move, because now they were all around me.

I knew my mother was waiting for me to get home, but the gang blocked my way. I felt something cold and bristly brush my ankle. It was their pig, rooting around my shoes as though it might uncover a potato if I moved my foot. "Get it away!" I shrieked.

"Rufus," said the little one.

"What?" I said.

"It's not an *it*, it's a Rufus."

The others began to move in closer, crowding me.

"Where you from, a uniform like that?" the smallest asked. I could see the tattoo of the black broken heart on his chest: they were Blackhearts.

"Hey—I know you," said the leader, a boy with long, natty hair, who wore a white peasant blouse and carried a stubby walking cane. "You run through Goat Square like you're afraid of your own shadow. People think you are from the other side of the river, but you're not. Just another girl from Jozseftown. You think you are too good for us, don't you?"

"You don't know me," I said. But perhaps he did, for I was looking about myself, worried one of my classmates might see me with them.

"Yes, I do," he responded. "You live alone with your mother. Your name is Petra K. You can't keep secrets in Jozseftown."

"I'm Abel," the little one interjected, stepping closer, taking his top hat off. He had dirty blonde hair, piercing blue eyes, and was in profound need of a scrubbing. "This is Jasper," he said of the large, mean-eyed one. "That's Isobel," he said of a dark, misty looking girl. She was bewitching, in a brightly woven shawl wrapped around her body. "She doesn't have a tattoo because it is against Half Not tradition, but she is still a member. And this is Deklyn, leader of the Blackhearts."

"I'm not allowed to talk to you," I said, which was true. "I need to go home." Again, I tried to duck from their midst.

"Not so fast, not until you buy something," said Deklyn. The boy would not budge. Nor would I. I may have gone to the Pava School, but this was my neighborhood, too, and his attitude made me loathe him and his dirty brow. I tried again, only this time I hit him squarely with my shoulder. I could see the surprise in his eye as I walked quickly away from the stunned group. It looked like they might follow me, but my escape was unexpectedly aided by the appearance of a large Half Not boy on the other side of the square. As if in imitation of the Blackhearts, he was holding small vials out to passersby. I recognized him as member of the Big Thumb Devils, a rival gang.

"Hey!" the one called Jasper yelled to him. I had been instantaneously forgotten.

"Come on!" Deklyn said, and took off to confront the boy, the others following. Only Rufus stayed behind, trailing at my feet until I too hurried from the square, toward home.

OUR HOUSE SAT ON A DARK and cramped side street, across from an abandoned marionette repair shop. It was an old, decrepit townhouse ornamented with grinning gargoyle friezes on the eves and a chipped wreath of granite roses above the doorway, appearing as though the house itself had been a living creature that was suddenly turned to stone. It was always shadowy, and even to me looked abandoned from outside, though I knew mother was home. I unlocked the door and listened. Behind the first door on the left lay my mother's room. Most times she was but a muffled and grave voice, beckoning me in for punishment or instruction.

I tiptoed past the door to her room. How long, I wondered, had it been since she had sealed herself away in there?

"Petrushka!" she called out, using her nickname for me.

I shuddered inwardly, took a deep breath, then twisted the brass knob, which somehow managed to stay the same degree of cold year round. I cracked the door and poked my head in.

"You are late," mother said sternly. She was lying in bed, as usual, and drinking tea poured from a pewter pot that was at her constant bedside service. "Have you been playing where you are not supposed to?"

By that, my mother meant *anywhere*.

"No. There was a cart in the square. A gang of boys was there."

"I told you not to associate with their sort. They can't even bathe in moonlight without turning it muddy."

"I wasn't *associating*. I was just *there*."

Mother always needed educating. No, let's face it, she needed help. But not in an obvious way. She would protest, and raise her eyebrow if you said anything intended to better her situation. You had to slip things in, like medicine in a sugar cube, so she could come around to things on her own. Though she usually didn't.

"Petra K, come here," Mother said. I took a cautious step into her room. The bed ruffled, extending from her like an enormous, worn wedding dress of a jilted bride.

"It's OK, come closer," she said when I had stopped at the foot of the bed. I moved around to her side. "Tuck me, dear," she instructed. I tucked in the sheets expertly; it was my daily chore. "Now give me a kiss and get me some more hot water." I kissed my mother's cold, pale cheek. "It's this neighborhood, dear. We shouldn't be living here. But because of that . . . man." By "that man" she meant my father. "That's why I keep you close. That's why I send you to a proper school though God knows we can't afford it. So you don't end up like that superstitious, devious man. No, I have said too much. Now go. Go clean yourself. I swear you are starting to *smell* like one of those little street thugs."

I reddened and at first felt shunned, then suddenly angry, then very lonely and sorry for the woman, who herself hadn't washed in weeks. Still, I wished I could stay by my mother's side for a little while longer, though I knew remaining would only bring more reproach upon me. So I swallowed my hurt and backed away, silently, measuring my steps to the door, then turned and ran, tears burning on my cheeks.

Later, only after I had cried myself out, did I boil water for tea.

Chapter 3

The next morning, the classroom reeked of the perfume Tatiana had taken from my bag. It was at the very least distracting. Though Miss Kavanova said nothing of it during the lessons, she did open a window. I tried to concentrate on the lesson, but kept wrinkling up my nose. One got used to even the strongest of smells, but this one didn't seem to go away, and it reminded me of Zsofia's rejection of me each time I inhaled. Not to mention that there was a strange tension in the room that I couldn't put my finger on. It felt as though there were some secret plan the others had set in motion. Just when that thought occurred to me, Miss Kavanova paused in the middle of our history lesson. "Is everything OK?" she asked the class. "Everybody looks a little green today." *Yes, that was it*, I thought. Everybody did have a slight green pallor to them.

"Fine, Miss Kavanova," said Tatiana firmly. "Now you were just telling us about some Jozseftown fairy tale."

"It is not a fairy tale, this is history we are talking about," replied Miss Kavanova sharply. "The Monarch, before his illness, recruited the best alchemists and scientists from the hovels of

Jozseftown to work for him in the Palace. Of course, there are stories of hauntings and curses still active in the ghetto."

"Creepy," said Sonia.

"Creeps*ville*," said Margo. Everybody looked at me. They all knew I was from Jozseftown. I don't know why we had to study it in class. Like I was some sort of living specimen.

"I think it is simply fascinating," said Tatiana. It was hard to tell when Tatiana was being sarcastic. But the fact that she took a knob of dry sausage from her purse and began to gnaw on it lent an unprecedented insolence to her comment.

"Tatiana," said Miss Kavanova, "put that away now! I have never . . ."

"Put what away?" said Tatiana, chewing rabidly. "Oh, this?" she said, looking at the greasy sausage in her hand, as if she did not know how it got there. Tatiana looked as genuinely astonished as Miss Kavanova. "Sorry, I don't know what got into me." The other girls giggled uncertainly, but were silenced by Miss Kavanova.

"Let's break for a few minutes. Take some fresh air and when you return I want your complete attention."

"Yes, Miss Kavanova," the class chimed in unison.

I stayed in my seat while the others filed out of the room. Miss Kavanova seemed momentarily lost in her consternation, before noticing me. "Go on, Petra K. You too." I left the classroom to join the others in the school garden. I wandered around the well-kept grounds, half-heartedly chasing the peacocks that lived there, gazing at the bushes pruned into sculptures, the bursts of violet and *tulipan* beds. Just once I wanted to see a bush that wasn't sculpted, a flowerbed that wasn't planted in straight, flawless rows. Then I would have a place where I would feel comfortable amidst all that stupid perfection. And, in truth, there was an occasion during break time in the previous year when I had actually kicked up a snapdragon bed just to create some confusion, only to find the plants precisely reordered the next day.

I wandered more. It wasn't until I rounded a porcelain cistern that I happened upon the rest of the class. They were hidden in an alcove of hedges, sitting in a circle, feasting ravenously on food they had brought. Sonia was ripping the flesh from a pickled pig's knuckle, Lenka had half a smoked chicken that she was tearing straight from the bone with her teeth, Tatiana was busy with another sausage, and Bianka, the kindest of the group, was apparently so starved that she had uprooted wild beet, the maroon juice running down her chin like blood. They looked like a band of savages, grease and pulp smearing their faces. Nobody even noticed me until Tatiana suddenly looked up. It was a look that I will never forget, one that was both predatory and defensive, as if they were birds of prey and I had stumbled upon their nest. But it was more than that: Tatiana's emerald-green eyes shown with pure hatred. Which was nothing new—she never made an effort to hide her dislike of me—except that Tatiana had *blue* eyes. Of this I was sure. But as each girl paused to look up at me it was the same. They all shared the same piercing, emerald-green eyes.

I backed away, then turned and fled.

In my haste I knocked into Zsofia, who had been walking toward me. As I picked myself up, I snuck a look into Zsofia's eyes. They were the same chestnut brown they had always been.

"Petra K," said Zsofia. "You are the only one I can talk to. You are not going to believe what happened."

"What?" I demanded.

"Yesterday, I followed the others until they agreed to give me a squirt from the bottle. But they sent me away after that, which was fine, because I had to get home for dinner anyway. My mother was so upset that I was wearing perfume that she made me go take a bath. In truth, I was feeling kind of funny anyway. Everything seemed sharper to me. And I was real hungry. All I wanted to do was go hunt down something to eat. You know, like actually *hunt* something down to eat it. It took all my self-control to draw a hot bath to wash myself. But when I was about to get in the water,

I caught a glimpse of myself in the bathroom mirror. What I saw wasn't me. I had scales, and fangs, and my arms were webbed with wings. I was changing into some kind of monster. But when I looked at my body, it was normal; it was just my reflection that was changed. I got in the bath and scrubbed myself until all that perfume was off me and didn't dare look into the mirror again until this morning."

"That's good," I said.

"No, it's not! It's so *disappointing!*" said Zsofia, her face falling.

"Why?" I asked.

"Because, I'm normal again," my former friend said blithely. "Now everybody has green eyes and I still have stupid brown ones. I never should have taken that bath. They won't even let me near them anymore. I'm missing all the *fun*."

"Wow," I said, impressed. "Do you think we will get out of school early today?"

"The chances are good."

The bell sounded, calling us back to class. When we arrived in the classroom alone, Miss Kavanova looked visibly upset by the absence of the others.

"Where are the rest?" she asked. I exchanged looks with Zsofia, unsure how to answer. We remained silent. Miss Kavanova's face reddened, and she began to twirl a lock of her hair with her index finger, which was what usually happened before she really lost her temper. But before she could exercise her wrath, in filed Tatiana, Lenka, Margo, Sonia, and Bianka. Their faces were clean of grease and beet juice, their uniforms neatly tucked in. The only thing that was different was the scent: it had grown stronger still. They must have besprinkled themselves again before retuning. My sleeve immediately flew to my mouth: the gnawing began in earnest.

Things were fine through mathematics, and half of our calligraphy lesson. But there was still a strong tension in the air. Miss Kavanova was putting on a show of teaching while the class was putting on a show of learning: what was really happening was that our teacher was keeping a vigilant eye on us, waiting for the slightest disruption or hint of unrest. But no real hint came: until Tatiana rose from her seat and walked calmly to the window. Without even looking back, out she jumped. The entire class was silent; even Miss Kavanova paused, standing as still as a statue: the window was on the second floor. Then went Lenka, practically sprinting from her seat and leaping out the window, followed by Sonia and Margo. Bianka was last. She paused on the windowsill, looked straight at Miss Kavanova, and opened her mouth. But instead of an apology, or even a curse, a jet of fire flew from her lungs, stopping right before burning Miss Kavanova's face. Then, she too jumped, leaving our teacher speechless and with singed and smoking eyebrows.

We got out early.

I ARRIVED AT SCHOOL THE NEXT DAY to find it closed. A proclamation hung from the gate declaring it off limits, on the authority of the Ministry of Unlikely Occurrences. I spent the weekend at home with my mother, cleaning the house. I scrubbed the floor tirelessly, as though I could scrub through to a different Pava, one where I belonged. Then, under the pretense of shopping for food, I went to Goat Square Market and put a coin into the metal hand of an automaton news vendor. I waited for it to slowly, creakily lift the kuna to its mouth, releasing a latch, which in turn let its potbelly fall open, allowing me to reach in and grab a newspaper. Thus, I discovered the fate of my classmates.

Strange Disease Overtakes Pava School

Yesterday in the Central Palace District a butcher's shop was looted by a gang of girls, whom witnesses claimed to be from the nearby Pava School. "I thought there must be a fire, or something like that," said butcher Pavel Polak. "A group of neighborhood kids came rushing into my shop like a red hound was chasing them. But, no, there was no one chasing them, and they didn't stop at the counter, scrambling right over it, almost like they were flying, and overtaking me. I shook them off as best I could then fled the store, letting them rip into the goods in the cooler. I could see them tearing into raw liver with their teeth, ripping chunks from leg of lamb, with crazed animal looks in their green eyes that I will not soon forget."

Polak then locked the store from the outside and alerted a patrolling Boot officer. He proceeded with caution when opening the door on the youngsters gone berserk. (He, like many others who witnessed the scene, swore the girls were actually flying around the room.) By his account, the group of girls did not rest until all the meat of the shop had been devoured, scraps of their rampage strewn across the walls and the windows smeared with grease. To subdue them, a mystic was summoned from the Ministry of Unlikely Occurrences. A tarp was hung over the shop's window and the Boot quickly dispersed any curiosity seekers. Over the course of the night the mystic was able to tranquilize the girls with a spell, then had them delivered to and locked in his workshop. After experimenting with various materials, he was able to concoct an antidote, and by the time dawn broke, the four perpetrators were released from his cellar, claiming not to have a single memory of what they had done.

The mystic, however, points to a black crystal bottle of perfume.

"Pure dragonka musk plus some standard flower essence. This kind of wickedness should not be allowed," he stated to this reporter. Though the authorities wanted to question the mystic more, he would hear nothing of it; his meditations had been disturbed enough. He disappeared back into his abode and was not heard from again. An investigation by the Ministry of Unlikely Occurrences is ongoing.

THAT THERE WOULD BE NO MORE SCHOOL in the near future did not stop my mother from making me wear my uniform and keeping it neat and pressed. Mother refused to put me in the local Jozseftown school, with its leaking ceilings and intense focus on the study of the occult.

With so much time alone, I was haunted by the question: who poisoned my classmates? And why? To be honest, a little embarrassment might have done them good, but there was also Zsofia to think about. The questions circled around my head like gnats. They just would not go away, and no toy could distract me from their buzz. Alone in my attic room, my play chest of toys scavenged from Jozseftown trash cans felt outgrown: the stuffed newts, automaton dolls that moved on their own, and crystal mood shards that lit up in the dark. I wound up my metal Kina-made dragonka, and watched it clatter toward me, its jaws opening, looking like a jagged, torn aluminum can, before it stopped and shot a weak flame from its mouth. But it offered no comfort. It was cold, like the house was cold, like my room and my mother's tea had grown cold. I picked it up, and disposed of it in the depths of my closet, deaf to its rattling and scraping.

I COULDN'T LET THIS THING GO UNSOLVED. I hadn't stolen the perfume that had poisoned my classmates. It wasn't fair, should I be somehow blamed for it. And fairness is one thing that you can contribute to the world when you have no power or money. I decided to start my investigation into the tainted perfume at Goat Square Market.

The market was crowded that day, and luckily for me, abuzz with talk of the strange occurrence at the Pava School. Over time I have learned that there are two types of news: the kind you read in the newspaper, and then there is the real kind, that can only be heard by hovering around the edges of crowds. It was there that you heard the true story: chatter passed from a greengrocer as he passed a parsnip to a waiting hand, or between two old ladies as they appraised the day's catch of eel.

"Terrible," one lady said, as she held a dried plum to her nose. "I hear the Palace is not pleased."

"I hear a minister's daughter is still afflicted, and ate the family cat when nobody was looking," her friend responded.

"Appalling," the first lady said, allowing a smile that said she was relishing the gossip, be it true or not. Tiring of chatter, I bought a poppy bun and sat down to snack. It was then that I noticed a crowd had formed around the Dragonka Exchange, across the square. In the ancient Exchange, fortunes were routinely made by buying and selling shares in the precious creatures. The dragonka, of course, were behind most mysteries Pava offered up. They were the source of the nation's wealth, as well as our living national treasures. The building that housed the Dragonka

Exchange was the pride of Jozseftown and shined like a single white tooth in a mouth of rotten ones.

I crossed the square to the Exchange, then pushed my way through the crowd, toward the newborn pup in the display case. I was only feigning interest, but after a moment, the dragonka pup's charm began to work on me, and I started to look at it with genuine affection. It was rutty gray with an iridescent sheen—most were like this, or a muddy brown or murky green: muted, unattractively colored until they reached maturity and their scales became radiant. The pup seemed to gather its courage, expressing its need to fly, even with a crowd looking on. But its wings were still not agile enough, and it merely fell onto the cedar chips that lay on the bottom of the cage. It poked its head up and sneezed, then stuck its pronged tongue out and licked its nose.

I had always longed for a dragonka. But the expense of one was well beyond anything we could afford. Owners spent untold kuna on their finicky diets alone, some dragonka resolving from birth to eat nothing but Ruskin caviar, others preferring the bitter chocolatey petals of the *orgona* flower. But foremost was the expense of the beast itself. Speculators had driven the price up so high that only a privileged few could afford any show-worthy dragonka. Even a runt could go for as much as a small house in the country.

Suddenly, a curtain was drawn across the display window. The crowd let out a sigh of disappointment, then, after a few moments, dispersed. I guessed I would hear nothing valuable of the so-called dragonka fever today.

It was then that I noticed a commotion going on at the main entrance of the Exchange. A Boot cart was there, and several officers were pounding on the Exchange door. It was highly unusual for the Boot to enter Jozseftown.

"In the name of Archibald, we demand admittance," one officer shouted. But no response came. It was as if the Dragonka Exchange had become instantly deserted. The officer pounded again, but still got no response. The Boot officer looked around in displeasure, then kicked the door out of frustration. "When we come back, we will not be so polite!" he shouted at the door, then jumped into his cart and whipped his horses into a fury, accidentally knocking over a pumpkin stand in his rush to get out of Jozseftown.

In looking for answers, I had only uncovered more questions.

Chapter 4

Later that week, late one night, I was awoken by a faint song. I got out of bed and peered out my small attic window, which looked out over the neighborhood. Dim paraffin street lamps burned through the misty air. Raucous drinking chants of people leaving the pubs, and the shouts of children playing late in the street, rose from the dark crevasses below. Somewhere out there, life was happening without me. I opened my mouth and hissed, in imitation of a dragonka. I wished I had doused myself with the perfume as well. My classmates had been on a wild adventure, due to me, alone in my attic—left out, even from tragedy.

Then I saw something curious. Zsofia, walking alone, through the streets of Jozseftown below me. She seemed to glow in a dull gold light, ghostlike. It was impossible. She lived on the other side of the river, in the Palace District. There was no way her parents would have let her out this late, to wander around alone in Jozseftown. I called out, but she must not have heard me, because she kept going.

I needed to follow her. Mother was most likely asleep, and if she wasn't, I would not be hearing from her until she needed her morning tea. I opened the window and, experimentally, stretched one leg outside. With my foot, I found the trellis where ivy grew, and discovered it could support my weight. Out I climbed.

The night sky was clear and cloudless. I could see well enough that my footing was sure as I climbed down the delicate wood framework, until I reached the street. But where the neighborhood seemed so alive from my window, now it was totally silent. I looked for Zsofia, but she was already gone, so I quickened my pace in hopes of catching up with her.

Most of the storefronts on Goat Square had already shuttered and locked their windows, the shopkeepers having retreated into their comfortable hovels to count the day's takings and eat meals of boiled pork and cabbage. The streets, once bustling with shoppers, were now deserted. A wind blew through the gates and arched passageways as though the neighborhood was emitting a great yawn and settling in for the night. Alone, I strode down a shadowed narrow street that wound like a serpent away from the square. I was cold, so I walked fast to warm myself up, keeping my eyes peeled.

Faster I strode—passing news automatons, eyes shut as though in sleep. The sound of Half Not fiddlers escaped the pubs, along with the sound of stomping feet. As I walked, a mist gathered around me, like it was trying to wrap me in its chill and billowy damp. It was crazy to be out in Jozseftown this late at night. Maybe it was true what superstitious residents said of the mist in Jozseftown, that it charmed the lone wanderer, misdirecting them, getting them lost in the mazelike warren of back streets and courtyards. I looked about myself. In a moment of panic, I realized I did not recognize the street I was on. There was a fountain, with a statue of a boy holding a fish, out of which a trickle of water spilled onto dead leaves. I had never been on this spot before.

Suddenly the copper gargoyles that hung with such poise from the gutters of the Tyyn Church appeared to move. One slithered down the drainpipe, its hungry eyes upon me. No, my imagination was playing tricks on me, I realized when I looked closer. It was simply a coil of ivy blowing in the wind. Then, in front of me, I saw a small, dark shape duck around a corner. I followed it, but when I got to the corner I found the street empty. I began to walk more quickly. The paraffin lanterns that lined the streets gave a warm orange glow to the cobblestone underfoot.

Again, all trace of Zsofia had disappeared. Now I was alone on the street that ran along the great Pava River. I gave up my search. Before returning home, I paused to see if I could spot one of the phosphorescent dolphins that sometimes sprang from the river at night, glowing like crescent moons. Instead, my eye caught a dark figure on a bridge, upstream from me. Even though the person was not doing anything unusual, they had a suspicious air about them. In fact, the figure appeared shadowy, as though their body was cut from dark, fine silk. I crouched down by the riverbank and observed. Indeed, the person looked around, then dropped an object over the side of the bridge, into the river. The thing bobbed in the water but did not sink, and the current was such that it was caught by a jetty and shot my way. It took no more than a few steps into the murky waters to grab the discarded object and rescue it before it was submerged in the black water. Pulling it from the current, I discovered it was a coarse burlap sack, tied at the top. I almost dropped it, because something inside the sack moved, then began to squirm terribly. Somebody was drowning kittens, or an unwanted hound pup. I pulled at the string to release the pitiful animal. I undid the tie, reached in and pulled out—to my disbelief, but at the same time, satisfying an unspoken expectation —a tiny dragonka hatchling.

I looked about myself. The figure on the bridge had disappeared, nor was there any other soul about. The street was empty but for me. The chill had evaporated from the air and the paraffin lanterns seemed to burn stronger now, lighting up the darker corners and cul-de-sacs. I breathed heavily, relieved, no longer fearful. Who was that person, and why had he tried to drown a small creature? *And why had fate intervened and sent it my way?* I had to ask this also, for behind small mysteries, especially in Pava, there often lie greater mysteries.

I hurried home. Now Jozseftown's charm appeared to be working in reverse, for every darkened street I took led me to a brighter, more familiar one, as though hastening my trip. In no time, I was outside my house, and climbing the ivy-twined trellis up to my room.

SAFE IN MY BEDROOM, I slipped the creature—sleeping now —from the sack and laid it on my bed. After I patted it dry with a towel, I examined my find. The dragonka was captivating: already some fluffy hair was growing behind its ears, the sign of premature wisdom, and its markings were inkblot shaped and well defined. I'd read enough to know that its true color would not become fully apparent for another half year or so, when it began to mature: a molting process during which it would sleep for a few days, then, upon waking, shed its old skin. I turned it over to have a better look. On its belly I found a sheen of gray-green, like the iridescent color of a green bottle fly. The pale green on its flanks and body were speckled with turquoise flakes like the verdigris of a copper coin plucked from a wishing well after so many years. I pulled one of its long, elegant wings from its body; claws small as thumb tacks adorned the ends, the skin thin and transparent, soft as the finest kid leather. It might become a fierce fighter when it grew up, though it had a friendly face that belied any violence.

But the beast was suffering. Its breathing came in fearful winces; the dragonka was still in shock. I wiped away a quicksilver-colored tear that leaked from its eye. I rubbed its belly in hope of giving comfort. It was then that I noticed a long ruddy scar that ran up its breast, as if it had been in a terrible fight. It instinctually wrapped its wings around itself, hiding the scar.

One thing I knew in my gut: I had to protect this dragonka. Some twist of fate had delivered it into my hands, and now it was my responsibility. Thoughts of my classmates would have to wait. I put them out of my mind just like that. I can be quite sinister when I want to.

I watched over the pup curled up on my pillow until I could keep my eyes open no longer. As I fell into sleep, I felt the first effects of the charm that dragonka exert over their masters. My dreams that night were not like any I had experienced before. It was like I was floating in a warm sea of spirits: not just the spirits of people, but of wild animals and dragonka, suspended in front of me in the bright chambers of my mind, chasing each other through rays of light thick as tree trunks. Great gardens of under-water flowers blossomed, their fruit both strange and hypnotizing. I shared a dream with the beast, though soon the color drained away, and I dropped into a deeper, dreamless slumber.

WHEN I WOKE FROM THAT STRANGE SLEEP, I realized I was already late with mother's morning tea. I took the dragonka, slipped it into its sack, and carried it with me to the kitchen. Placing the bag on the kitchen table, I busied myself boiling water. By the time I cracked the bedroom door, mother was awake and sitting up-right in bed, looking at me with an icy gaze.

"You are late," she said.

"Sorry," I said.

"You are not," she replied.

I tried to place the hot water on the bedside table, but keep-ing my attention on mother, should she lash out. In my careless-ness, I misplaced the pot, and it went tumbling onto the floor. But my mother did not explode. It was as though she had willed or expected me to fail at such a miniscule task. There was a look of satisfaction on her face.

"Now clean it up," she said calmly.

I ran back to the kitchen, retrieved the mop, and began boiling another kettle of water. By the time I had finished cleaning, and remade mother's tea, I had almost forgotten about the dragonka pup. I rushed back to the kitchen and looked in the bag. The dragonka was no longer there.

I looked behind the furnace, checked under the table, searched out the lightless space behind the pantry, but the pup was nowhere to be found. Soon, there came a whimpering sound from atop the tallest kitchen cabinet. Balancing a chair on the kitchen table, I was able to reach the top of the cabinet, where it had escaped to, looking like one of the stray vampire bats that sometimes took shelter in the house's eaves. On the bright side, I now knew I had a flyer. And a hungry one, I could see. To tempt it my way, I offered forth a handful of poppies, but it turned its snout up haughtily. I searched the kitchen and found some oats. But again it refused, as it did with dried apricots and figs. Finicky little thing.

"Fine," I said. "Then you just won't eat at all." But upon voicing those words, the dragonka's features brightened. It was the first time I had spoken to it, and it was pleased. How *aggravating*.

I collected the pup, taking it from its perch, and put it back in its burlap sack. I quietly left the house by the front door.

Chapter 5

The streets of Jozseftown were already bustling with activity. A troupe of Half Not children, led by a dwarf fiddler, pushed their tin collection cup in front of the faces of tourists, while others snuck up from behind and picked their pockets. Morning shoppers crammed the poppy dealers, buying mounds of black seeds in cones made of newsprint. Stalls selling sweet honey and fig rolls did brisk business, as did vendors selling fiery fruit brandy made of quince and imported mandarin oranges. Automatons clattered about on two legs or wheels, some in human form, some robotic animals, collecting coins in exchange for a song or a fortune. On Goat Square, an ox had gotten loose from its minder and was charging passersby, upsetting maps stands, and terrifying tourists. Just another day in Jozseftown.

When I retrieved a paper from the corner automaton, I learned some shocking news. The "dragonka fever," as it was being called, had spread beyond the Pava School. Ludmilla's outlet shops from as far away as South Mikulov were accused of selling goods tainted with the transformative musk. A sanitarium had been set up in the Black Forest to cure and rehabilitate the stricken. Archibald the Precious had ordered all Ludmilla's shops closed and her employees quarantined. There was even a connected story of a dragonka abandoned by its wealthy owners for fear of their children's health. The reaction was unprecedented.

Perhaps that was why somebody had tried to get rid of the beast; discarding it like a prize treasure that they learned was nothing but a piece of costume jewelry. As if it sensed it was under consideration, the pup began to squirm in its sack. I could feel its tiny claws against my chest as they poked through the material. I took it from my pocket, but before I knew what was happening, it burst from the opening, flailing its wings, then falling to the ground in front of me like some failed version of a flying machine. I went to pick it up, but it scampered from my grasp. I stooped over to grab the errant beast, but before I could get it, it darted from my reach, scuttling between my legs and out of the passageway, barely avoiding being hit by a passing pretzel cart. I followed, but when I reached the square the passageway opened onto, the dragonka was nowhere in sight. I looked this way and that, but there was no sign of it.

Then, from nowhere, appeared three Blackhearts, lined up in front of me. The beast was clinging to Abel's chest, shivering. I became immediately shy; I felt embarrassed to be caught out, unable to keep the dragonka under control, as though I had failed in some unstated mission. But, unexpectedly, when I saw it in Abel's grip, I felt protective. I wanted it back.

"Hand it over!" I said.

"What?" said Jasper.

"Maybe she wants something to rid her of that dragonka fever," said Deklyn. "She does look a little scaly today."

"Give him back!" I said.

"This runt?" said Jasper. "He'll never win any tournaments. Best you can hope for to get money out of him is if you sell his hide to a wallet-maker."

"I don't want money from him," I said.

"But isn't that what these dragonka are all for?" asked Jasper. "You know there was a time when real dragons ruled the sky. Only a chosen few could ride them. But—for the sake of profit—the powers that be turned them into these ridiculous little toys. What a waste."

"Big deal," I said.

"Oh, did they teach you to behave like that in your fancy school?" said Deklyn.

"What do you know?" I asked.

"A lot," he said.

"I'm sure you do. I bet you work for the Boot," I said.

"What?" said Deklyn. "Why would you say that?"

"Because you sell fake potions and nobody arrests you," I said. "Everybody knows the Boot has spies, even here."

"I have lived in Jozseftown all my life," he answered. "The neighborhood protects me, and I protect it. We have nothing to do with the Boot. Nothing. *Never.*"

"Fine," I acquiesced.

"Give the princess back her toy," said Deklyn, whom I was beginning to really dislike. Who did they think they were? But Abel seemed unwilling to relinquish the dragonka. He looked back and forth between me, Deklyn, and the small beast. He finally walked over to me and held it out.

"Take good care of it," he said.

The dragonka flew from Abel's hands into mine. It was still shivering, but calmed in my embrace. I turned from them and stalked away, anger burning in my cheeks.

BUT THAT WAS ONLY the beginning of my troubles. That night, when I was quietly playing with the pup in my room, I heard a pounding at the front door. I tiptoed down the stairs and listened to my mother shuffle from her room. She opened the door a crack, but it was quickly thrust open by a huge, black-uniformed arm. The Boot.

"Citizen," the officer began in a stern voice. "We have come to check each pet for dragonka fever. Please present any beast in your household to us at once."

"But we have no dragonka here," my mother said. I could hear fear in her voice. But it was not a lie, for she still knew nothing of my pup.

"That is not what our sources tell us," said the Boot.

"Look at us," she said. "We are poor. How could we keep a dragonka?"

Please, I silently begged Mother, *do not fail me here.*

The Boot faltered. He knew she was right. Probably he issued the same command at every doorstep in hopes of catching out some poor soul.

"Very well," he said. "If you see any suspicious activity in the neighborhood, or any unclaimed dragonka pups, please let us know. Archibald the Precious is very concerned." I let out a sigh.

"Is that all?" Mother asked.

"If you have no beast, then I am afraid I will have to ask for any gold you have in the house," he responded formally.

"Gold?" she exclaimed.

"Yes. We are to confiscate all gold. In the name of the Palace."

"But I have no gold!"

"We can see that is not true," the officer said.

"You can't mean . . . this? It's my wedding ring!" she cried. The silence that was followed by the soft shutting of the door confirmed what I knew: she had given them her ring. I felt a wince of guilt: I was responsible for that somehow.

IT WAS TIME TO START MAKING SENSE OF THIS. The next morning I again tucked the beast into its burlap sack and made my way through the crowd toward the Dragonka Exchange. The dragonka perked up as we neared the market. It could sense other dragonka behind the gates, and became alert. Traders from the Exchange came and went through the building's darkened door, which was arched and heavy like that of a castle. Reliable accounts had it that the gate led to another farther on that opened up upon a courtyard. There, the Exchange's private stock of dragonka were kept, the flying ones exercising their wings and the earthbound dragonka frolicking beneath. Their stock of dragonka, used for breeding and research, was rumored to be unparalleled. It was the source of limitless wealth, the breeds of the dragonka collection unmatched in variety and rarity.

I ARRIVED AT THE HEAVY DOORS and banged the knocker, which was fashioned to look like the nose ring of a horned dragon. A guard peered out at me from a small portal.

"Yes?" he demanded sternly, as though I was a beggar.

I did not know what to say, but before I could even speak, he slammed the window shut, after shouting "no visitors!" I knocked again. This time, when the latch flew open, I took the dragonka from its sack and held it out for the man to see.

"Well then," he said. "Here for a sitting? That is another story."

Dragonka owners were each entitled to a sitting with the Exchange mystics, who rated them on characteristics of coloring, poise, and charm, thus determining their price on the open market.

I walked in the now open door, gazing around. The entranceway was adorned with friezes of dragonka, which lined the walls like hieroglyphs, telling the story of their domestication from great ancient Dravonian dragons; of how the Dragonka Exchange modified them over the centuries until they were the pet dragonka we know today. Traders brushed past me, hurrying to and fro. "You just wait here," the guard said. Before long he returned with an escort, a snippy little man dressed in a sharp suit with an identification badge hanging from his neck, who would take me to the mystics. As we passed the doors to the courtyard I could hear the Exchange's dragonka as they played and exercised. My dragonka heard it, too, and craned its head in their direction.

"The mystics are quite occupied today," he said. "So don't be surprised if they dismiss you. This way." He was obviously busy and wanted to get rid of me as quickly as possible. He led me down a long flight of stairs, then sat me down on a velvet sofa opposite two iron doors. The doors to the sitting room creaked open and a voice boomed from inside. "Enter!"

I picked the beast up and passed into the darkened room, which smelled of incense. The door closed behind me; I faced a jury of three identical mystics sitting behind a huge wood table.

"Don't be afraid," said one. They were aged men, long gray beards hung over their black tunics. "Put the creature on the table in front of us, then have a seat." I had a list of questions I wanted to ask—but fell immediately speechless. I did as I was told. The dragonka promptly went into a pout, curling himself up into a ball. No sooner did that happen than the center mystic reached out and grabbed him. I felt my heart protest at the rough way he was being handled. This was a surprising feeling. Where did that pang come from? But the creature submitted, allowing the mystic to unfurl it and hold it stiff as a board in front of him, like a stuffed fish.

"A problematic one, this beast?" the mystic asked me.

"Yes sir," I responded. They passed it from one to another. Not one betrayed a hint of approval or dismay. They put it back on the table, then leaned in to confer. This lasted several minutes, until they broke and fixed their gaze on me.

"Perhaps we should keep Luma for the evening," one mystic finally said. "Just to get a more thorough appraisal."

"Luma?" I said.

"Yes," laughed the mystic. "This is your dragonka, isn't it? He does belong to you?"

"No," I admitted. "It, he, is not mine. That is why I am here."

"It doesn't matter," said the mystic. "Owning something is about paper and words, things with no power. Luma *belongs* to you, and that is different. Don't you agree?"

"Yes," I answered. *Luma*, it sounded nice to my ear, and seemed to harmonize with the dragonka's ethereal and dark demeanor. How they knew this, I could not tell. That is why they were mystics, after all. The dragonka, upon hearing his name, jumped up and scampered about the table, from one end to the other. The mystic produced a bag filled with pellet-sized reddish fruit, pinched some with his fingers, and held it out to Luma, who devoured the food voraciously.

"He's eating," I said.

"Pomegranate seeds. You can never go wrong with pomegranate seeds."

Luma spun himself in dizzy circles then came to an abrupt stop, falling over.

"*Moody little thing*," commented the oldest mystic. Then suddenly the door to the room was thrown open.

"What is the meaning of this interruption!" demanded one mystic.

The guard at the door looked stricken.

"It's the Boot," he finally said.

"Tell them to go away!" the mystic bellowed.

"I cannot. They are stopping all dragonka trade," the guard stammered.

"What? The Boot have no authority here," shouted another mystic.

"I am afraid it is even worse," said the guard. "By Archibald the Precious's order they are removing the dragonka. They are closing us down. We have to get you away. Quickly, through the catacombs."

Forgetting about me, the three mystics rose and rushed from the room, moving stealthily and nimbly for men so aged. The dragonka—*Luma*—immediately jumped to my chest and clung to me. From outside the door, I could hear the sounds of shouting, dogs barking, and the braying of dragonka. I snuck up the steps and peeked around the corner. There I saw Boot agents who, with their black uniforms and red wolfhounds, were streaming into the courtyard, carrying metal cages and nets. They were returning with dragonka, which were crying in high, wretched sounds that sent shivers to my core. I watched as dragonka traders were marched out of the building, their hands bound. Boot guards beat old men with their batons in order to get them to move faster. When one dragonka tried to escape, a noose was cast around its neck, and it was pinned to the ground and held there until it was unconscious on the floor.

I tucked Luma into his sack and hid it under my coat.

I walked down the corridor. Boot agents flew past me, in search of the Exchange's hidden vaults and chambers. I walked through the mayhem unnoticed. Near the entrance, I saw that the door to the courtyard had been flung open: the private stock of the Dragonka Exchange exposed. I could not resist peering inside.

There I beheld a sight as dazzling as a firework display's grand finale. Dragonka of the most unique breeding and coloration were swirling about in the air in prismlike beauty, while the earthbound ones were jumping up on their hind legs, in an effort to evade the hounds of the Boot. The dragonka were enthralling, like deep-sea fish. One had a tiger's coloration and markings, others were tiny and delicate as butterflies, and hovered curiously in front of my face for a few moments before moving on. Muses of *kiš*-dragonka (dragonka in miniature, no bigger than lightningbugs) swarmed through it all, stressed by the upheaval. A panicked dragonka scampered past me and charged the front door, where Boot agents were waiting with huge nets.

"Let none escape!" yelled a Boot commander. Guards seemed to be everywhere now, throwing furniture from the upper stories of the courtyard, making large piles of sales receipts and deeds to pedigree, and setting them ablaze. Then suddenly a huge red wolfhound was upon me, barking in my face, its teeth yellow and dripping with spittle. This was the first time I had been close to a red Boot hound, its fur raised on its back, blood-lust in its black eyes. It could have bitten off my arm as easily as one would pull husk from an ear of corn. I recoiled. The hound, sensing something concealed, sprung at me. There was nothing I could do but pretend I had lost my mind and play along. Without thinking, I was five years old again, playing dragonka, flapping my arms, pretending to breathe fire.

"I'm just a poor dragonka," I said, running in circles. "What will become of me?"

The officer who clutched the dog's leash looked bamboozled, his net held in mid-air. Fear, he expected. Idiocy, no. Then something else caught his attention. "Get it!" yelled the Boot officer. The dog crouched as the officer threw something in my direction. A spiked net came flying at me like a bird of prey. I ducked and over my head it went. The massive dog followed, leaping over me, its claws grazing my scalp. I turned and saw that the net had ensnared a snarling dragonka with boarlike tusks, now cowering under the dog's barking. I took the opportunity and dashed quickly from the Dragonka Exchange, with nobody taking further notice of me.

Being peculiar has its advantages.

ONCE OUTSIDE, I could see cages of dragonka being loaded onto carts, drawn by draft horses decorated with the black and red colors of Archibald's regime. But in the rush and confusion, not all the dragonka could be caught. The fiercer ones evaded the nets and dogs and were escaping into the maze of Jozseftown's streets. The Boot made no move to capture them, instead concentrating their efforts on closing the Dragonka Exchange. I took cover behind a pastry seller's cart across the Square and watched.

Before I had time to take in what was happening, a strange carriage chugged into the Square. It was long as a riverboat, but puffed up and squash shaped, and looked to be made entirely of bronze. The vehicle was accompanied by a squadron of armored horses and Boot officers who ran alongside. The parade came to a stop in front of the routed Dragonka Exchange. A uniformed driver rushed from his place in the bronze carriage and opened the back passenger door. A man—no, it was a child!—stepped gingerly from inside. It was Archibald the Precious himself.

Archibald the Precious looked about as though he was in a savage foreign land, at once interested but a bit shocked by its level of filth. Boot officers cleared the way as he strutted over to the cart carrying the confiscated dragonka. He walked the length of the cart, gazing at them greedily.

"That one," he said, pointing to a gorgeous stark white albino Sibernian dragonka. "Oh, and that one too," he said, indicating a huge purple dragonka with a fish fin that ran down its back. "And that one! And that one over there! Splendid. Prepare them all. I want them all!" Archibald exclaimed. The officer nodded, made a motion to the driver of the cart, and it was off. Archibald licked his lips and surveyed the square. His gaze stopped near me. He dispatched another officer to appropriate a choice honey and poppy roll from the cart I was standing behind, then hastily retreated to his vehicle, which again puffed steam into the air, churning on its own locomotion as it drove away.

ARCHIBALD, THE MONARCH'S SON, had become a source of both speculation and fear amongst common Pavains. After the Monarch's rapid decline in health, and recent death, the boy had assumed power with a rapidity and ferocity that amazed most observers. Nobody knew exactly what his age was, but he did not look much older than me. Rumors about the man-child had abounded for as long as I could remember. It was said that he only had the appearance of a wizened child, but was actually quite aged. Other stories told of darkened carriages with exiled enemies of the Monarch being ushered into the palace gates late at night; of crypts being opened and ransacked for their scrolls of the dead, of bizarre experiments of reanimation and alchemy taking place in the basement dungeons of the Palace, all under the supervision of Archibald and his Ministry of Unlikely Occurrences.

What was known for sure was that Archibald's enemies were disappearing from the streets, and those who openly opposed him found themselves imprisoned in cages hung from the trees that lined the road to the Palace, kept like wild animals where boys could throw pebbles at them. Under Archibald the Precious's influence, the Imperial Seat was taking a tighter grip on the citizens of Pava; newspapers that were previously critical of the government were shut down, their editors sent into exile in Sibernia. Tourists were thoroughly checked at the border and those without proper documentation were turned away. Even people in the markets felt less free to speak to one another when it came to the rise of Archibald the Precious. Only hushed tones were used, and only with those who could be fully trusted. It was known that Archibald had already engaged the use of spies amongst Pava commoners, and those overheard speaking ill of him would disappear in the middle of the night, never to reappear, or if they did, they were profoundly altered, as though a spell had been cast over them. For all this, Archibald was becoming widely feared.

AFTER HAMMERING A BOARD over the entrance of the building, a Boot commander addressed the crowd that had gathered. "The Dragonka Exchange has been deemed the source of all dragonka fever. The Dragonka Exchange is henceforth closed and quarantined. Any citizen found to be trading in dragonka will be subjected to arrest and reeducation. Your shops will be closed, your homes razed, your families impoverished. Dragonka—as you know them—have been deemed a national health hazard. All breeding and showing of dragonka is henceforth forbidden under direction of Archibald! All stray beasts shall be turned in to Boot Headquarters for processing, and all pets shall be officially registered with us. Nobody shall pass the gates of these walls from this day forth. We appoint this spot to erect an information board, where you will be updated on our future policies regarding the dragonka." With that, his underlings raised a bulletin board on wooden posts, hammering through the cobblestone.

From across the Square, I could just make out the figure of Deklyn, watching the completion of the raid. For just a moment, our gazes met, then he looked away defiantly, before turning and fleeing the scene. Luma had instinctively gone limp, as dragonka sometimes do under extreme stress. I quietly made my way home, the noise of the Dragonka Exchange's pillaging falling silent at my back.

Chapter 6

From that time on, things became a little darker in Jozseftown, as if a thunderstorm was hovering just above, bursting with rain. The neighborhood was quieter, only sometimes a Boot cart would come rumbling down the street, filled with net-carrying officers, chasing a stray dragonka. I watched these chases from my window, like taking in a cheap shadow puppet show. Passersby would stop what they were doing and make bets on who would prevail; sometimes shopkeepers would hide the dragonka amidst their goods. But, of course, there were instances when the Boot would get lucky, and emerge from an abandoned building with a sorrowful looking dragonka caught in their net, flopping about like a fish out of water. The beasts were thrust into the back of a Boot cart and never seen again.

But there was more to it. Lingering in the Goat Square, I heard stories of dragonka trading hands within the walls of Jozseftown. The rich were bringing their beasts and selling them to foreign traders or exchanging them for small quantities of kuna. Suddenly there were all these strangers in Jozseftown, carrying dragonka under their coats like illegal firearms. The Exchange still existed, it had just gone underground.

I THOUGHT THAT PERHAPS if I hung out around the markets, I might spy the dark figure who had dropped Luma from the bridge. Nothing unusual happened the first night, but on the next evening, while I was pretending to look over some old shrunken beets, I saw a well-dressed man half-heartedly browsing the vegetables, looking embarrassed and awkward there in the ghetto. He stopped at a notoriously unscrupulous greengrocer, who handed the man a slip of paper, after the exchange of a few coins. Following this, the man consulted a map, then began to make his way down one of the dark causeways that extended from the Square like tentacles. Perhaps he could lead me to the source of the illegal dragonka trade.

I followed the man, keeping to the shadows. His unfamiliarity of Jozseftown was obvious, as he kept stopping to consult the map. It was frustratingly slow, as I needed to get home to make my mother's evening tea and check on Luma, who was nesting behind the shut door of my closet. Eventually, the man came to the address he was looking for and slipped inside the vestibule. It was the storefront of an abandoned pharmacy, the gilt letters peeled off by scavengers for their gold residue.

I approached the dark building. The window was dusty, and I could not see in. I took a brave step toward the door, and was about to open it when I was surprised from behind. "Who's that lurking about?" came a voice. I spun around. I was often accused of lurking, even when, in my opinion, I was merely strolling furtively. Though in this case I was definitely lurking.

In front of me was Jasper, the biggest and meanest of the Blackhearts. He looked me up and down, as though unsure if I was for real or some mirage. "What are you doing here?" he demanded. His blonde hair flared from his head like a lick of fire.

"I heard you were snooping around the Exchange as well when the Boot raided the place."

"Don't look at me like that. I . . . I am on your side," I said, unsure of what I meant.

"It doesn't matter which side you are on. In fact, it is better if you are working for the Boot. You may have the others fooled, but I know who you are. I see through you. And you are dangerous," Jasper said.

Jasper brushed past me and entered the pharmacy. I heard the sound of a lock being fastened behind him. I didn't know how to respond. What can you say when somebody states your worst fears about yourself?

I ARRIVED HOME LATE; the smoky smell of my mother's tea hung in the hallway as I entered. Had she prepared it herself? That would have been real progress. I breezed into her bedroom without knocking to discover that she wasn't alone. She was surrounded by Boot officers. No, they weren't exactly officers. It took me a few moments to believe my eyes: there was Tatiana, Lenka, Bianka, Margo, and Sonia all dressed in Boot uniforms, sitting around her as though visiting a much-loved, or dying, relative in the hospital. They turned toward me, their faces displaying a strained expectation, as though I was a party guest whom everybody had been waiting on just a little too long.

"My, my," Tatiana said, looking me over. "Who do we have here? That school uniform is very last month," she said, with a wink that just might have been playful. Could it be Tatiana actually missed me? Now that I had a chance to take them in, I could see that it was not actually a Boot uniform they wore, but the uniform of the Boot Youth Guard, as evinced by a patch each wore on their arm. Gone were the gem-studded bracelets and black-pearl necklaces. Instead, each girl had a pin ornamented with a golden eye stuck to her jacket lapel. But even in this stiff uniform, Tatiana looked fashionable. She just had that way about her.

"Petra," said my mother, suddenly alert, or perhaps, afraid, "your friends stopped by to say hello."

"Where have you been?" Tatiana continued. "You are going to have to start the program from the beginning, but maybe when you catch up, they will put you in our troop."

"What troop?" I asked. "What program?"

"After we were cured of the fever, we were put in the Youth Guard Facility to recuperate."

"But what about your parents? What about your dragonka?"

"Dragonka! Ha!" said Sonia disdainfully. "Rats of the sky."

"Perfect them by and by," the others chimed in unison, as though it was a poem they had been taught to recite.

"What are they teaching you there?" I said, perhaps a bit too incredulously.

"The truth!" exclaimed Lenka, with an uncharacteristic zeal for learning.

"The teachings of the Number One Play Pal," said Sonia.

"What is that?"

"Archibald. Number One Play Pal. We are learning the rules of the game," Margo said.

"Fair and square," said Sonia.

"No dragonka there!" the others rejoined.

I swallowed, though my mouth was dry. These were not the girls I had known from the Pava School. No—they were—only there was a blankness to their eyes, and their words came mechanically, as though they were part automaton.

"Where is Zsofia?" I ventured.

"What, you didn't hear?" Lenka said, suddenly springing to life.

"Shhhh . . ." hissed Tatiana. "Zsofia—"

"You can come with us now," said Tatiana. "We have a bunk for you and everything."

"Besides," Lenka commented, "your mother tells us she can't even afford to feed you anymore, now that all her money was lost in the closing of the Dragonka Exchange."

I looked at my mother; she averted her eyes and took a sip of tea. It was true that she hadn't given me money for food in many days, and we had but scraps remaining in the cupboards. Even worse, I was concealing the fact that I had picked fruit from a garbage bin by Goat Square Market to feed myself.

"And," said Sonia, redirecting my attention, "your mother said it was OK if you came."

I looked at mother again, but her face revealed nothing. She had her tea and her bed.

"OK! I'll be right back," I said, with forced cheer. "I need to pack."

"I'll go with you," said Margo.

"No," I said, perhaps too quickly. "My room is a mess. I'll just be a minute."

"Don't be too long, Strangeling," said Tatiana with her trademark wink. She was the only girl who could make a wink look threatening.

I dashed up to my room and began to pack: I tucked Luma into his burlap sack; I grabbed a handful of sunflower seeds for food, and slid out my attic window. It was the first time I had escaped my room in the daylight, but aside from the few doves I scattered from the window sill, nobody took notice of me as I scaled the house's façade.

I disappeared into the streets of Jozseftown, questions swarming about my mind. What were my classmates doing in the Youth Guard? Why their sudden hatred of the dragonka? Why had they come to find me? More importantly, how long would I have to wait before I could go home? I unexpectedly felt envy for the Blackhearts. They had no parent to answer to. They knew how to get by on their own.

I WANDERED UNTIL IT WAS DARK. I was hungry again. I would have to pick through the over-ripe and damaged fruit the vendors left behind at the end of the day if I wanted to eat. But quickly

I realized that I was not the only one with this idea. Other figures, ghoulish and pale, were furtively poking through the bins, coming back with half-eaten morsels. I found a promising looking bin in a remote corner of the food market and began to rifle through its contents, coming up with a still-edible cauliflower, a handful of quinces, and a packet of poppy seeds.

Then—from nowhere—a voice emerged from the darkness.

"Did you find anything good?" It was a small child, hiding in the shadows.

I rummaged around in my bag and found a ripe quince, then passed it into the shadows. The hand reached out and accepted the food. I heard a quiet munching come from the darkness, then silence.

"Thank you," came the meek voice.

"You're welcome," I said. I was about to ask the child who he was (the truth is there were more and more orphaned children seen in Jozseftown these days), when I spotted Abel across the square. But I restrained myself from shouting out to him. There was something sly in his movements, like he didn't want to be seen.

"I have to go now," I said to the child in the darkness, and started after the Blackheart. Abel was, I can say, sneaky as a cat. He seemed to disappear in shadows, then reappear on the other side of the street altogether. But I managed to keep up, and soon enough we were at Goat Square. Abel slunk along the storefronts, then, after looking around, pulled the door to the Dragonka Exchange open and slipped inside.

Maybe my curiosity got the better of me, maybe I just wanted to prove I was a better sneak than any Blackheart, but I followed him. At the Exchange's door, I noticed the nails to the boards the Boot had shuttered the entrance with had been pried loose, and replaced with hinges, so that it still looked closed. The Exchange was still being used—but what for?

I was intent on investigating, but Luma was growing more restless under my coat. Something was exciting him. In the entrance hall I tried to hush him, but suddenly there was no controlling the creature: Luma burst from my grasp, and sprinted toward the doors that led to the courtyard. He began scratching at the wood. Before I could grab him, those huge wooden doors cracked open, and Luma dashed through. I moved quickly, but was immediately drawn up short by what I saw there. The courtyard was packed with people: dozens, if not a hundred spectators were standing in a circle, cheering. At the center of the ring I could see two dragonka pups prancing around in circles, as though they were chasing each other's tails. And, it turned out, that is exactly what they were doing: circling pylons in order to overtake the other, then administer a bite on their opponent's tail, ending the race.

"Welcome to the League of the Maiden and Minor Pup," said Abel, who had materialized behind me. "Not sanctioned, highly illegal, but you can make a lot of money here. Come on, let's watch the races!"

"But Luma," I began.

"He is safe here," said Abel.

I followed Abel deeper into the room. Nobody took any notice of us as we pushed our way to the front of the crowd. The audience was composed of all stripe of Pavain. There were black-clad, bearded Zsida sharing a bottle of red wine, arms around each other and loudly cheering on their favored dragonka; there were Half Not gangs issuing bets. Some in the audience had come in formal dress, and there was more than one anonymous, masked observer. I could see the other Blackhearts too: Isobel and Jasper, as well as a few members of the Big Thumb Devils and Stink Clovers, pitting their dragonka against one another.

"I don't have to tell you that this is a secret," said Abel.

"I'm good with secrets," I replied.

"I know," said Abel. "That's why I let you follow me."

"What is this?"

"Different things to different people, I guess," he said. "Dragonka breeding is just in our blood here. You can't post some stupid sign and expect people not to show off what they've got. Then there are the Half Nots. If you gave them good enough odds, they would bet the sun wouldn't come up in the morning. So there is money in it. Some of these people are foreign scouts who want to take our stock while the price is cheap. Plus, it's good for the dragonka. They need the attention. Without a chance to be seen and fawned over, they either mope about or start raiding the markets for food."

"And what is it to you?" I asked, though I really wanted to ask what it was to *me*.

"It's a laugh," he said. "Something to do. We are laying off on the potions for a bit while Deklyn works his new plan out, so it gets kind of boring around town."

"But aren't you afraid of the Boot?"

"Naw, they'd never come into Jozseftown at night. Too dangerous. Plus, we're careful."

"Yeah," I said, though I had stopped listening. I was keeping my eye out for Luma, whom I still couldn't spot. "I shouldn't be here, should I?" I said, suddenly apprehensive.

"No. It is totally unacceptable. But no need to worry. If anybody asks, just say you're with me, Abel Blackheart," he said, throwing open his shirt, revealing the black heart tattoo.

"Do you guys always have to go off showing your silly tattoos to everybody?"

"Silly?" Abel said. "Deklyn inked this into me with his own hand. This has the ancient charm of pure Pavaian River clay mixed into it. That's how I knew you were following me through Jozseftown. I can tell trouble from a mile away."

"I am trouble?" I asked, half-offended, half-proud.

"The worst sort," said Abel. "But I don't mind."

I needed to find Luma, but before I could search further, I was interrupted by a commotion on the floor. The two racing dragonka had gotten into a fight after the winner nipped the loser's tail with too much enthusiasm. Soon they were a tumbling ball, whirling around the room, a blur of fangs and scales into which nobody dared intervene. This caused another sudden wave of betting, this time on the results of the fight. I watched the brawling dragonka spill into the spectators and the crowd surge back. To distract the audience a Half Not band started up, playing on spoons and blowing jugs. A troop of Sibernian soldiers began dancing a high step, and some celebrants took the opportunity to settle old scores—I saw a pocket picked, a cup of mead poured over a woman's head, and more than one fistfight break out; and for a few minutes the room was pure chaos, like a wedding party that had been overrun by a riot.

Suddenly, the audience regrouped, as another competition had begun, and the issue of betting needed to get underway. I was pushed into the midst of the crowd, and was beginning to panic because there was no sign of Luma anywhere. But the ferocity of the spectators' cheering retrained my attentions to the pit and the two dragonka racing around it. It took me a moment to believe what I was seeing: Luma was one of the racing dragonka. And from the looks of it, he was winning.

I shoved my way to the first row, all the way up to the perimeter of the pit. Luma was moving quickly as a ferret around the ring, chasing the tail of a dragonka pup that looked like a squat lizard, its tongue hanging from the side of its mouth in fatigue. It was not long before Luma inflicted his bite on the other beast, which let out a high-pitched whimper before scampering from the pit. There was a collective groan from the crowd, as it seemed Luma had been heavily bet against. I noticed only a few cheers, the loudest being from one of the Blackhearts. There I saw Deklyn collecting a purse of kuna from the Half Not bookmaker.

I pushed my way over to him. As I did, a Half Not attendant delivered my panting dragonka to Deklyn's arms. The Blackheart held Luma, stroking him behind his ears. I immediately felt an anger rise in me. When Luma sensed me there, he immediately fluttered from Deklyn back into my arms.

"What are you trying to do?" I yelled over the noise.

"What do you mean?" he replied casually, tossing his bag of coins from hand to hand.

"With my drangonka? With Luma!"

"Luma," said Deklyn, trying the name out on his tongue. "I like the name, maybe we will even keep it."

"*You* will keep it?" I was so angry that my words sputtered like a misfiring engine.

"This creature never belonged to you. I don't know where you got it from, but it's not yours. I asked around after we saw you," he said, reaching into his pouch. "Have a few kuna for your trouble." But I knocked the brass kuna from his hand.

"He *belongs* to me," I shot back.

"You? You can't even take care of yourself. And see how lean Luma is? That is not right. Even a racing dragonka needs a little fat to fire his breath with. You haven't even trained the beast to do *anything*."

Deklyn was right. And though I could barely feed the both of us, I would find a way. But I wasn't going to admit that. Not to him. We both fumed at each other for a few silent, unhappy moments before the Half Not girl spoke.

"Stop it!" Isobel commanded, stepping between us. "It is obvious that we need each other. Listen," she said, turning to me, "we need a beast of trainable age. There just aren't many left, with all the quarantines and confiscations. And you, well, you need to survive. Deklyn is right. We know all about you, and your mother, and we have seen you hitting the bins at night. You might survive, but the dragonka can't. Not on picked-over corncobs and stale poppy buns. Luma obviously belongs to you. That much anybody can see. Nothing will change that. But we can be partners in his training and share his winnings." She turned to Deklyn. "That means cooperating."

Deklyn grunted something I could only take as grudging acknowledgement. "She is Luma's master, but we all have to take care of him, *if*," she said, grabbing the pouch of money from Deklyn's hands, "if this is going to continue." One thing I noticed right then was that when Isobel spoke, Deklyn listened. "Plus," she continued, "the Boot has been looking for our lair for weeks now. It is only a matter of time before they find it. The beast will be well-hidden in Petra K's."

"OK, OK already," Deklyn said. "But she has no idea how to train a dragonka. That is where we will start."

"You can talk to me," I said. "I'm right here."

He turned toward me as though I was some sort of night-sprouting fungi that had popped up without warning. "You have no idea how to train a dragonka, and *you have no idea what you are getting yourself into*."

All eyes were on me. I realized then that I had at least *some* power over them. And, I have to admit, despite my distaste for Deklyn and his gang, what Isobel was proposing excited me. More than anything I wanted to escape my mother's oppressive silence. And that we might actually make some money, despite the danger, made it an irresistible offer. "I don't care," I said to Isobel, just to spite him. "Tell him I agree. Luma and I are in."

"Fine," Deklyn sputtered. He obviously did not like being ignored either. "Eighty-twenty split with the winnings."

"Eighty-twenty?" I spat out.

"There are more of us," he said. Jasper, Isobel, and Abel were all standing behind him now.

"Seventy-thirty, plus you bring me pomegranate seeds for Luma," I countered.

After a moment, Deklyn nodded his assent. He signaled to his gang, and they began to depart.

"Hey," I shouted at him. "Thirty!" I held out my hand. Deklyn shrugged, counted a percentage of Luma's winnings and handed it over to me. It was more money than I had seen at once in my entire life. I grinned, rubbed Luma on the back of the ears, and left the Dragonka Exchange.

Chapter 7

The next day I went shopping. I bought a shiny brass cage for Luma, with a feather pillow to sleep on, and a portable nest that fit in my coat pocket. I loaded myself down with poppy-honey buns by the stack, porridge and molasses to sweeten it, sticks of dried bison meat and jars of jam in every flavor imaginable. I visited the tea merchant and picked up tins of jasmine, and smoky oolong tea for my mother. I had been neglecting her. At home, I made her a small feast and carried it in to her room. She must have known I had been sneaking out, but she never let a word slip. But I could see worry crease the sides of her eyes. Those lines had grown like unspoken sentences over the weeks. If she voiced them, would they disappear, like words in the air?

I put the tray down in front of her but she would not look at me. She just poured a little cream into her tea and watched it cloud up, then stirred it briskly with her teaspoon.

I began to leave, but my mother called me back when I reached the door.

"Petra K, come here." I did as I was told. "It is time you knew. I have protected you for too long."

"Know what?"

"Look under the bed, Petra K," she said. I did. It was dark and musty but for a wooden box, which I pulled out.

"Put it on the bed and open it, Petrushka."

I did: inside I found—a *doll*? No, it was more like a small, intricately designed automaton. I took it from the box. It was a man with a foxlike face and sly eyes, dressed in a black silk cape.

"Do you have a coin?" Mother asked.

"A what?"

"A coin," she restated. From my pocket I drew a brass kuna.

"Hold it toward him," she instructed. I offered the coin slowly to the automaton. But before it got close, the money flew from my hand. It landed in the open palm of the doll, which activated a gear, and the coin was passed into the sack. The doll had stolen my coin! I laughed with glee.

"That is what I was worried about," said my mother. The trick did not please her, nor did my reaction.

"What is it?" I asked.

"That, Petra K, is Jozsef K. That is your father." I looked at her, stunned. The *doll* was my father? "He wasn't a tea trader. That was a fib I told you. Oh, he liked tea. He could steal bushels of it out from under the best-guarded Indyn caravan. He could steal the wheels of a cart while it was still moving. That is what your father was. That is why you never spent a day in the Jozseftown school, because he was so notorious that even the teachers knew of him. Amongst thieves he was legendary. The Thievery Guild had this made in his honor once he disappeared. I wanted to keep all that from you, in the hopes that you would be different."

"He disappeared?"

"See what I mean? You only hear what you want to hear." She sighed, took a sip of her tea, then set it down on the bedside table.

"But you just said he disappeared, so how do you know he is dead?" I asked.

My mother grabbed me. I did not know if it was out of love or anger—then I realized, by the intensity with which she was holding me, that it was both. Though it was suffocating in its firmness, I savored her touch. I could feel hot tears from her cheeks burst against my neck. Then she whispered in my ear, "I know he is dead, because I have seen his spirit."

On the topic she would say no more.

For the first day of training, Isobel met me on Newt Island, which sat in the Pava River in between the large and small sides of the city. By decree of an ancient treaty, Newt Island was a place free of Imperial authority, and was safe from the Boot Guard, at least for now.

"Where are the others?" I asked.

"We don't need them. We will be training Luma in the Half Not way. It is subtle, and demands great gentleness and concentration. Deklyn and the boys would just get in the way."

Isobel's *fazek*—her Half Not costume—had been redone in a bright, striking design, like that of an ornate Persian carpet. It was legend that rare Half Not girls were born with wings, which were a source of great embarrassment for the parents. These girls were forced to wear the woven fazeks that hobbled the wings beneath the yarn, making them deformed and unusable, for a Half Not girl who could fly away would never be found again—such was their wanderlust.

"Are those really wings under that yarn?" I asked impetuously.

"Don't concern yourself with things that aren't your business," said Isobel, giving me another sharp look. "Let's begin," she said.

"Begin how?" I asked. This question only proved my ignorance of Half Not ways. They rarely responded to such direct questions. Isobel only stared at me blankly, leaving me stung by how unfair it was to forbid me from asking questions. It was as if she was training me, not Luma.

"The trick to real dragonka husbandry is not to make the dragonka conform to your behavior but to find a way to make their own nature flourish. You have to find the individual characteristics within the dragonka and bring them out into the open for the entire world to see: this is the artistry. This is a Half Not talent." Isobel demonstrated what she meant by whispering Luma's name on the breeze. Soon enough the beast perked its head up, then trotted over to us.

"Now sit," she instructed me. "Look into each other's eyes." I did, gazing deep into the coal black pits of my dragonka's eyes. How strange to acknowledge his own particular existence and soul.

"This is called spirit breaching," Isobel told me. "It isn't enough to just feed and pet the dragonka; there needs to be an exchange that can only come in this way." Indeed, after a while—like when you repeat a word enough times—I began to forget who Luma was. First he was just a pair of dark glossy eyes gazing back at me; then it was as if Luma was being re-born in front of me, like a seed drawing nourishment from the soil. How difficult to recognize the intelligence behind Luma's eyes as different than my human one, but somehow not inferior—and what a crime it would be to try to dominate and exploit that intelligence. In the face of this, the past and future disappeared: there was just a live being, whose body harbored every bit of love and timeless cold passion in the universe.

The young Half Not broke the spell after a period of time that I could not measure.

"It was a good try, but watch this," said Isobel. She repeated the exercise, gazing into Luma's eyes with her own. But after only a few minutes she broke the spell. Isobel put my hand to her chest, then put my other hand over Luma's heart. They were beating at the same pace.

"It is how my ancestors used to travel with so many horses," Isobel said. "Driving a herd across all Dravonia and not one horse lost, because they moved as one creature, with one heart. You cannot fully train a dragonka without knowing how to master this." I wrapped my loden cape tight around myself and nodded. "You see, all these wizards and potion-makers like Deklyn, they think magic is something you force into the world with ingredients and spells. But that is not the Half Not belief. Magic, if there ever was any, comes from inside. And it is in everybody, not just a chosen few. That is the real practitioner's secret."

We stayed in the park until late, having lost track of time. Though Isobel made attempts to master Luma, he still displayed a strong will against ownership. After I tried again to spirit-breach with Luma, Isobel ended the session.

"It is taxing for him, and you," she said. "Let's relax now." She passed me a bottle of elderberry juice, gave me a handful of pomegranate seeds to feed Luma, and then pulled a violin from its case. When she began to play a strange, eerie tune, Luma immediately perked up, and, like a dog howling at the moon, began to sing in a high-pitched, atonal braying. Before long, a few other dragonka, who had also been surreptitiously hiding in the park, came out of their refuges and joined the chorus. Suddenly, I could see the notes of the song hovering there in front of me. They were colored: deep lavender and purple, fuchsia and crimson, and colors wholly new to my experience or to this world, colors that must remain unnamed. I felt calm, and for the first time since the dragonka fever, happy.

I HAD ARRANGED with Isobel to bring Luma to the Half Not ghetto later in the week, so that we might continue training him for the tournaments. I rarely came here, and felt particularly unsure as I entered the neighborhood.

The buildings in that part of Jozseftown were mostly grand, decaying tenements that gave the impression of jigsaw puzzles that had lost a few pieces over time. While I was gazing up at one, a group of Half Not children chasing a chicken almost knocked me over, then I was spun around again by the clanging of the elaborate but dreadful astronomical clock that kept time in days, weeks, centuries, and millennia according to the planets rather than breaking time down into pesky seconds, minutes, and hours. The place itself was making me dizzy. I teetered, about to faint. Then, from behind, a hand landed on my shoulder. I looked up: it was a man cloaked in a long black overcoat. The brim of a hat shadowed his face, but in his hand I could see he held a cane, the top adorned with a carved dragonhead.

"Do you know that that clock above us has over ten-thousand moving parts? If but just one does not function perfectly, the clock cannot tell time." I looked up at him. Though he smiled at me, it was a salesman's solicitous, insincere smile.

"So like a heart, don't you think? Two perfect contraptions, one of metal and the other of muscle. But both take spirit," he continued. "I used to make clocks. But now I am concerned with matters of the heart."

"Excuse me, sir," I said. "I am late." I started to walk away.

"Child," he said with urgency, stopping me. "Where did you get that beast?"

"What beast?" I responded. Luma was safely concealed in his portable nest in my jacket.

"I can feel it," he said. "You have a dragonka, and an exceptional one at that." I looked around. There was no one who might help me should he cause trouble.

"I don't know what you are talking about," I said.

He chuckled. "You know it is now illegal to even keep a dragonka, much less train one."

"I'm late," I said. "My mother is waiting for me."

"Here," he said. "There is no reason why we can't be friends." He held out a sack in his hand. He shook it so I could hear the jingle of coins inside. "I will take the beast abroad, where it will be safe. There are kings and land barons who would take great care of him. And in return, you shall have enough gold to move from this decrepit place." It struck me that I was dealing with a dragonka trafficker. The kind who sold beasts to foreign dealers as pets, or, if rumor was true, as a delicacy in fancy restaurants. I noticed the strong smell of camphor coming off him. There was something terribly wrong about him. Luma, too, began to squirm against my chest.

"I have no dragonka," I said, "and if I did, I would not send him abroad. Not for any price."

At first, he did not appear to register my response. Then, he opened his cloak: there, from the fabric, I could see the sleeping bodies of six dragonka stitched into pockets. He then took his cane, and tapped it firmly on the cobblestone. At contact, the dragonka head came to life, eyes glistening, its mouth opening in a fierce growl. "I can take your dragonka in body or spirit, if you refuse. But I advise you to take the gold. Perhaps you can even buy your way out of trouble with the Boot, which is surely headed your way."

The dragonka staff began to let out a high-pitched wail, like the crying of a huge muse of dragonka. It was unbearable. I put my hands over my ears, then hid my head in my hands. Then—as quickly as it had emerged—the sound stopped. I opened my eyes to find myself quite alone. On the ground where he stood, I saw a piece of paper. I picked it up. It was a calling card. Written on it was one word: *Wormwood*. The man himself had vanished, as if into thin air.

I WAS EXPECTING TO MEET all the Blackhearts by the broken fish fountain, but only Isobel was there. Under the icy glow of the moon, I could see her true beauty for the first time, as though it was only revealed at night. Her black hair was sleek like a slice of ebony, and her eyes were almost impossible for me to look at without feeling a spell was being cast from them.

Isobel escorted me past Half Not betting galleries and pubs: The Golden Well, The Basilisk and the Bull, and The Stone Pillow, all full in the middle of the day; then she led me down more unfamiliar streets. She stopped in front of a dark alleyway.

"You first," she said.

"Here?" I exclaimed, stalling. But Isobel only met the question with her usual icy stare. Was I about to have my throat slit and be left for dead in some dark forgotten spot? I was not sure I trusted the Half Nots. In Pava, there was no such thing as a Half Not, just a "dirty Half Not." I fought against that prejudice, but now suspicion crept back in. No, I would not enter the alleyway, not for anything. I would go home to the comfort of my mother and a cup of tea. I opened my mouth to say something, then closed it again.

I went ahead of Isobel into the dark Jozseftown alleyway.

Chapter 8

"Keep going," Isobel said firmly.

Down the alleyway I ventured. *How many innocent tourists had been tempted into traps like this never to return?* I wondered, occasionally craning my head back to catch a peek at Isobel.

"Why are you taking me to this stinky place?" I asked.

"It is for everybody's safety."

We came to a great wooden double-door at the end of the alleyway. Two faces of horned demons decorated the doors; iron rings the size of horseshoes hanging from their noses.

Isobel reached around me, grabbed one of the nose rings, and banged it against the wood. After a few moments the doors creaked open, and a Half Not with a moustache greased into fine spikes greeted us. Recognizing Isobel, he threw the entrance open. I took a step back: the cavernous room was packed with people.

"Hurry," urged the host. "You never know what Boot spies are about." I looked at Isobel. I still had time to flee. Instead, I ducked quickly through the doorway.

"What is this place?"

"The Dragonka Exchange, reborn," she answered.

THE COURTYARD WAS FILLED with all stripe of dragonka and their masters. I could see a few mystics hurrying to and fro, arms full of folios and old books, and silhouettes of people toiling in candle-lit rooms.

"Here we are," said Isobel. Luma was fighting to escape my grasp, so I set him on the ground.

"But why are we here?"

"Didn't you see the post? On the board outside the old Dragonka Exchange?"

"No," I said.

"All dragonka ownership is now illegal. They have outlawed it totally. This is the only safe place to train Luma."

There were other dragonka I recognized from the League of the Maiden and Minor Pup being run around pylons or navigating a floating obstacle course. My gaze automatically tracked Luma as he scampered across the courtyard, frolicking with a larger, lavender-colored dragonka.

"We must be extra careful," she said.

"But why are they doing this?"

"It is the dragonka fever. They want to cull the entire species, to eradicate it."

"But where is this sickness? You only read about it in papers."

"They say it is affecting the countryside, but that is not true, because those who come back on caravans have nothing to say of it."

"Luma!" I called, a sudden feeling of dread overtaking me. But Luma was occupied, and would not come. "Luma!" I called louder. Isobel put her hand on my shoulder, silencing me. Isobel whistled gently, whereupon Luma immediately perked up and returned to our sides.

Then we got down to work. There was a lot to be done. To hone his coordination, Luma had to be trained on a levitating obstacle course of small gas balloons that were tethered to the ground. Isobel ran him through the drills: I felt a petty envy in the way she had total control of him. When she commanded a turn, he responded. When she whistled him to stop, he bounded to her side. *Her side!* I could feel my jealousy grow. Luma was "mine," even if we were sharing the booty of his winnings.

"Let me try!" I said.

"You are not ready. Luma may depend on you, but he doesn't yet respect the bond that is there."

"I am ready!" I stammered. Isobel's black eyes flashed in anger, then dulled. She stood back and let me take control.

"Luma, up!" I commanded. The beast looked at Isobel, then back at me. "Luma, up!" I repeated, taking a pomegranate seed from my pocket and holding it in front of him.

"That is not a good thing," Isobel began. "You will spoil him that way." But I paid her no mind. I wasn't going to let a Half Not girl, with her stupid jingly *fazek*, tell me what to do.

"Luma," I commanded, "fly! Go!" I dropped my hand as I had seen Isobel do, and to even my surprise, Luma was in the air, navigating the course. Only this time, he was flying at a pace far beyond how he had raced for Isobel. He tore around corners, spinning in the air, barely recovering.

"He is not racing," Isobel said. "He is just speeding through the course to get the pomegranate seeds." Indeed, he was missing his marks, and he veered wildly, colliding with another training dragonka mid-air, sending them both tumbling. When they hit the ground, the larger one attacked Luma, going for his neck with his whiskered jaws. Luma rose in flight again, the two squaring off like boxers.

"Luma!" I beckoned, but he would not come. Instead he let the other beast attack, dodging its bite, and inflicting one of his own on the passing dragonka's tail. This incited the larger one even more, who immediately took off after Luma. A chase ensued, despite Isobel joining the call to bring Luma down. There was nothing to be done. After another skirmish, the other dragonka pursued Luma through a second floor window.

With no time to bicker, Isobel and I sprinted up the building stairs and down the hall. We listened at the doors until we heard a commotion behind one, and thrust it open.

Upon entering, five faces looked at us in surprise. At first I thought we had stumbled upon a burglary, then I realized that we were witnessing something very secret. On the floor there was a great map of Pava, detailing the streets that led to the Palace. But also, I noticed a stack of iron weapons in the corner and a stock of bayonets, broken down and oiled. An old hand-operated printing press smelled freshly inked. Bottles of potion were resting in crates in the corner, their contents emitting a soft green mist. One boy was busy trying to subdue Luma and the other dragonka, while the rest were shielding the weaponry from the rumbling dragonka. On the wall hung a banner with handwritten scrawl that read: JOZSEFTOWN RESISTANCE MOVEMENT.

Suddenly, I was pushed from behind and fell into the room. Then the lights went out.

WHEN A CANDLE WAS LIT, the first thing I saw was Deklyn's face, a few inches from my own, his eyes piercing and full of rage. His breath came heavily, smelling of cabbage and night air. At once, it seemed like we were both orphans, like he had taken me into his world of street life—for all its adventure and loneliness. He needed comfort. It didn't matter if it was me, or Archibald, or anybody, Deklyn would push back when pushed. It was all in his eyes.

Then Luma flew to me, breaking his gaze.

"What is going on here?" I said.

"It is not for you to know," said Deklyn.

"Come," said Isobel, ushering me from the room.

"It would be best to forget what you saw," she said.

"But what did I see?" I asked. In her usual fashion, Isobel kept quiet. We ended training for the night, and I did not hear from Isobel until the next tournament.

Chapter 9

Even though Luma was mine, I still hadn't made any progress in answering my questions about him. So the next day, I took a walk over to the Karlow Bridge, to the spot where I had seen the man throw the beast over the side. I looked out over the Pava River at the swans that clustered around the riverbank. Above me, on one side of the Bridge, loomed the Palace, dark clouds hovering there year-round. On the other side of the bridge was Jozseftown, and the man hadn't come from Jozseftown. Something about the Palace repulsed me; it was so old and foreboding, like some bitter old woman full of scorn. I instantly felt that if I really wanted to investigate, I would have to go there.

I started off toward Palace Hill. I didn't know what I hoped to find, only that there *was* something to find. On the way up the narrow street that led to the building, I saw in the distance that huge metallic ornaments had been hung from the trees. It was only when I got closer that I realized they were not ornaments, they were cages. Inside, prisoners begged for water or food. I stopped in my tracks. Beneath their shivering bodies, my former neighbors strolled, ignoring the desperate pleas of their fellow citizens. These were the same people I had lived amongst when we resided on the Palace Hill. A bolt of shame shot through me. Or maybe it wasn't shame, maybe it was awakening, like a dark, night-blooming flower opening its petals.

I understood that the differences between people were enough to provoke cruelty. The differences between me and my classmates, the differences between the Boot and the clerics. This would never happen in Jozseftown, where everybody was—in their own way—an outcast. From my pocket, I withdrew a dried apricot, and tossed it up into a cage, feeling sorry and ashamed that I didn't have more to offer.

LIKE I SAID, I didn't know what I was looking for. With that in mind, it was quite easy to find things that seemed important. The front of the Palace was well guarded, but one could walk around back, even lean against the gray granite of the palace walls, which I did, cocking my head toward the sky, wishing for one ray of sun to come down and warm me. It felt like lingering at the backdoor of a haunted house. Then suddenly, I did feel warm—though there was no sun. It was a nice feeling, for the brief time I was able to savor it.

"Who's that, lurking about?" came a voice. I spun around to find a Boot guard approaching.

"Please sir," I said, putting on my most miserable pitiful beggar voice. "Just a crust of bread. And some jam. *Quince* jam. And a walnut."

"There is nothing here for you," he said. "Now get on out of here."

I did just that, but the warm feeling remained for a little, like a lantern I carried with me as I traveled. I *had* discovered something, because what I felt was the unmistakable charm of living dragonka behind that wall.

THE NEXT DAY MY MOTHER asked for a second helping of cream for her tea. I couldn't tell her that the money had already run out, just as the cream had the day before. Instead, I ran from the house and used the last of my winnings at the Goat Square market to buy it for her, and spent the rest on pomegranate seeds. As for myself, I would have to wait for nightfall to eat, when the trash bins were full again.

One thing I knew: Luma needed to win and win big. The next tournament was to be held underground and in the dead of night, such was the fear that Boot agents were closing in on the illegal events. Isobel waited for me at the broken fish fountain, which had become our regular meeting place.

"Where are we going?" I asked.

"Right here," she responded. But we weren't *anywhere* as far as I could tell, except standing on a deserted street corner. Isobel looked around, then bent down and with her stubbly, clawlike fingers, pried open a sewer grate over which we were standing.

"Don't worry," Isobel said. "I know the way. We won't be harassed."

I stopped myself from asking, "Harassed by what?" I did not want to know the answer.

We used a metal ladder to lower ourselves down into the dank, dark sewer.

"I can't see," I said. At least I did not have to worry about Luma, whom Abel had brought to the tournament earlier that day, "to prepare," he had said ominously.

"Stop complaining," responded Isobel sharply. I hadn't thought I was complaining; it was so dark that I had to reach out and test the space with my foot to find the ground, and could barely see an arm's length ahead of myself. When we both arrived safely on the ground under the brick tunnel, Isobel began to whistle an atonal tune, which she followed by a chanting that echoed off the walls and seemed to travel by itself down the passage. She was beckoning somebody, or something.

I kept quiet and waited. Soon a lilac-colored glow came from the end of the passage, like a candle that was floating toward us.

It moved slowly, drawn in by Isobel's summons. As it approached I saw that there was no flame at all, only the light, surrounded by wispy mist.

"It's a glow cloud," Isobel said. "There's a piece of lightning trapped inside the cloud, unable to find release. Created by magic refuse washed down the drains of long-dead sorcerers. They are basically friendly, unless they are too old."

"What happens then?"

"They begin to rupture, and like an old light bulb, they explode. You don't want to be around when that happens. Lightning gets everywhere," she said as if she were talking about spilled ink. "Come," Isobel commanded. The glow cloud obeyed, leading us down the ancient brick passageway. We continued on through the musty-smelling place, breathing air that had been still for hundreds of years. The cloud stayed faithfully by our side, occasionally letting off a slight muffled thunder. Once we had to stop as it rained briefly. Before long we arrived at a cavernous room. Isobel explained that it was once an event room for the Urban Druids, a long-disbanded association that was briefly seated in Jozseftown.

All the usual suspects were there, their dragonka ready for the races. We found our places in the competitors' box. There, I recognized members of other gangs, some dressed in scavenged and moth-eaten formal attire, in imitation of the elegant Dragonka Balls that were the mainstay of society before Archibald the Precious had them banned. I searched the floor for Luma and the Blackhearts, but could not spot them.

"What now?" I said impatiently.

"Watch," Isobel said. "The festival will begin, and Luma is up first in a mock joust."

"What is that?" I asked.

"Two flying dragonka circle each other in the air baring their teeth, making horrendous faces as they stalk one another. The point is to try to get the other to bite first. It is an exercise in self-control. It is in a dragonka's nature to attack, so the one that can be mocked long enough without cracking wins. We call it the Mock Joust of the Minor Pup, because Minor Pups are the newest, uninitiated dragonka."

As though on Isobel's command the Half Not with a greased moustache—whom I remembered from the Dragonka Exchange—came out and quieted the crowd.

"Thrill seekers one and all, I ask a warm welcome for last show's winner in the Mock Joust of the Minor Pup: Pikatrix." A jade-colored dragonka trotted into the circle. "We expect great things from Pikatrix, who will be facing a pup making his debut in our league: give a hand to Luma the Illuminator!" The lights were cut, and a spotlight was trained on the ring; I watched my dragonka led into the ring by Abel. Luma had been adorned with sparkles that made his natural sheen blaze like he was covered in tiny diamonds; for a moment he looked like matter from a star might if it was sanded off and rained from the sky.

"Luma!" I called reflexively. "What is he wearing?"

"Shhhh!" commanded Isobel. "It is a cheap trick, but that kind of thing goes over well with the audience. Besides, we need to hide that hideous scar on his chest."

I watched Luma circle the green dragonka, and then at the crack of a whip the two competitors rose in the air, their wings carrying them above the heads of the crowd to the higher reaches of the cavern. I had never seen Luma navigate his space so well, rising in a perfect spiral with precision that was elegant and practiced. His training had paid off. The two dragonka ascended facing each other, squaring off like street fighters, or ballroom dancers. When they reached the appropriate height, Pikatrix began to bare her teeth, her sharp gleaming fangs visible from where we sat below. Luma was not intimidated. He circled, keeping his eyes on the other dragonka, then made a sudden, violent dive at her with an open mouth in a mock attack.

"That was close," said Isobel. "If Pikatrix had moved toward him, his teeth might have caught her, which would mean a loss. Pikatrix is good, but she is afraid to let herself get hurt. Luma senses it, he is that cunning." But things took a turn for the worse when Pikatrix spread her wings, which were long and had a birdlike appearance. Her eyes blazed red. I watched Luma begin to cower. And a scared dragonka was sure to lose control. Then Luma caught my eye. The beast was suddenly braced. My presence fortified him. He turned back to the other dragonka with a renewed concentration. Luma too opened up his wings, expanding them theatrically, mimicking Pikatrix's movements. And, if it is possible for a dragonka to laugh, that is just what Luma did. This did not please Pikatrix, who tried to puff her chest out, but Luma only imitated this, too, and suddenly the crowd was roaring with laughter. It was an unusual, but very artful tactic, one that favored the smaller dragonka. This teasing was more than Pikatrix could bear, and she struck out at Luma. One bite, two, Luma dodged, then let the other attach her jaws to his protective leather collar. The whip was cracked again and Luma was deemed the winner.

We wasted no time watching the remaining matches. Though the festival was secret, the crowd was celebrating the return of the dragonka to competition. There was a tension in the room: people were guarded. Anybody could be a spy for Archibald and the Boot. It was safer to take our winnings and depart.

Deklyn led us through the sewers until we arrived at a room that was dank and humid as an orchid hothouse. The warmth came from huge metal pipes, beneath which piles of blankets were laid out as beds. Stacked against the walls were crates of the tiny vials, which I recognized as the potions the Blackhearts sold on the streets, a faint green radiating from them. Tools and the gears of a half-assembled dragon automaton lay in the corner, like a fallen soldier waiting for surgery. Jasper began sorting through a box of tiny metal levers, searching for the one that would fit his metallic patient.

"Where are we?" I asked.

"It's our home," said Abel. "Above us are the Zsida mineral baths. These are the hot-water pipes. That's why it's always warm here."

"Have a seat," offered Deklyn, indicating a place in an old rocking chair next to a card table. The others took seats as well, Deklyn in a large wooden chair whose arms were ornamented with dragonka carvings. He took the pouch of coins from his jacket, poured it out onto the table, and counted out my share. From his earnings he passed Abel a few coins, then whispered something in his ear. Abel nodded and left the room.

"What are you doing?" I asked Jasper. I knew he didn't like me, but he was happy to show me his creation.

"It's a model replica of Ruki Mur," he said.

"What is that?"

"Ruki Mur is the mother of all Pavain dragons. She was worshipped before the guilds decided to make lapdogs of her children."

"I thought that was just a legend," I said.

Jasper looked at me like toads had fallen from my mouth when I spoke.

"That is what you get for going to school," he said. "Lies and pretty stories."

"And you are going to ride Ruki Mur when she comes back, I suppose," I said, having a hard time not letting the contempt for his superstition seep out.

"Look," he said, turning toward me angrily. "They may trust you, but I don't. So just keep out of my way."

To avoid creating further discomfort, I left Jasper to his tinkering. By that time, Deklyn had divvied up the winnings. My stack of coins was waiting for me on the table. It was even more than the first tournament.

"Don't let this money spoil you," said Deklyn. "Other competitions won't be as easy." I kept silent: none of Deklyn's superior, snotty comments were going to keep me from feeling pride over Luma's victory.

"Where is the next one?" I asked.

"Nobody knows," said Isobel. "They are kept secret until the last minute to provide for maximum safety. But we will contact you in due time."

I noticed that I was being treated differently now. I was needed here, in this dank place under the city, a world away from the Pava School and its pristine beds of flowers. This was a new feeling, and I liked it.

By releasing a valve on the pipe and letting steam hiss into a mug, Isobel was able to make us hot ginger tea. Deklyn brought out a tin of dried figs, pickled eggs, and nuts and we shared a modest meal in silence. Before long, Abel returned. Over his shoulder, he was carrying a bouquet of *tulipan*.

"Over there," Deklyn instructed. Abel set the flowers down in a corner. Deklyn must have noticed the embarrassment on my face, because he was quick to point out that they were not for me. Jasper let out a burst of mean laughter. I felt a strange shot of resentment for the slight, then jealousy rise unbidden in me.

"Who are they for, then?" I asked. Certainly not Isobel. Even casual friendships such as the one the Blackhearts shared with the Half Not girl were viewed with disdain.

"She wants to meet your girlfriends," teased Jasper.

"OK," said Deklyn. "If we are going to be partners you might as well see how we live. Let's go, just leave Luma here."

"Where are we going?" I asked.

"Special delivery," he answered, picking up the flowers. "Come along if you want."

I paused for a moment, then my curiosity got the best of me. Again I followed Deklyn through the underground passages.

"Have you always lived under the baths?" I asked. His intentional mysteriousness was beginning to annoy me.

"No. The Newts took care of me for a while, but I am a child of Jozseftown, so I prefer to live here."

"And the others?"

"They all have their own stories. Jasper, for instance, came from St. Cecelia's."

"The orphanage?"

"Yes. But it is more like a prison to those who live there. And if you stay too long, they recruit you for the Boot, which might sound nice for somebody like Jasper, but the orphan recruits all get sent to the southern marshes, where they work in the sulfur mines."

"And Abel?"

"Nobody knows. Not even him. He just showed up one day wandering around the streets of Jozseftown, with no memory of who he was or where he came from. We had to name him ourselves. Abel: an ancient Pava hero, you know."

"I know," I said.

"Of course, you went to school. But where does your schooling get you down here?"

I had no real answer, so I just scoffed. From there, we walked in silence.

Before long, a strong smell of something like rotting vegetables began to overtake me. It was accompanied by a faint but definite sound of singing. As we continued along the corridor, the stench of the place intensified: we arrived at an opening and I could see an enormous cavelike room, at the center of which light from street lamps streamed in through a hole from above, illuminating the small mountain of trash that dominated the space. I could see childlike creatures scampering over the mess. They would wait for another bundle of trash to fall from above, then compete with each other in picking out rusted metal and bits of food, throwing whatever was unusable down a sewage canal. In the corner an old Victrola phonograph was playing.

"Kubikula," Deklyn said.

"I thought the Kubikula were just a legend," I responded. In history class we had learned the story of a race of prisoners of war that had been sentenced to life underground. It was said they had evolved into stubby, scaly, monstrous creatures.

"Where do you think your trash goes? Straight down here, in exchange for the Kubikula not rising up, or raiding markets after hours. True, every now and again a dog or goat disappears from above, after which you can smell cooking meat rising from the sewers, but mostly they keep to the pact."

"So what do you want with them?"

"We," he corrected me. "You are in this too now."

"We," I said, liking the sound of that word, despite my reeking surroundings.

"I have known the Kubikula since I was small. They are good to have on your side, because nothing that gets thrown out in this city escapes their notice. And they are hoarders by nature. You can find almost anything in their storage rooms."

"And what are we looking for?"

But before he could answer, a small Kubikula ran over to us. She obviously recognized Deklyn, as she threw her arms around him. The Kubikula was just a child, but she looked so much older, her skin pale as alabaster, and limbs stocky from being hunched all the time in cramped underground spaces.

"Here you go, Sytia," he said, calling the girl by name. No sooner did Deklyn give her the flowers than other Kubikula began to crowd around, putting their fingers on the petals, pulling the stalks toward them to get a better smell of the bouquet.

"That's one thing that never gets thrown out: fresh flowers. Come on," said Deklyn. "Soon they will have devoured them, and we will become the next most interesting things." I followed Deklyn into the Kubikulas' inner sanctum. We passed chambers that were filled with spare metal scrap, chambers with piles of dead flower petals, chambers crammed with animal bones. Finally we came to a back room where there was nothing but paper piled high to the ceiling. Deklyn immediately began to rifle through a stack. I plucked a piece of parchment from the top of one of the piles: it was a deed to the ownership of a dragonka. Somebody had just thrown it away, perhaps out of shame or guilt, to rid themselves of the evidence of something they had once held dear. Heaven only knows what happened to the dragonka itself.

"Those come by the dozen, these days," said Deklyn, taking the paper from my hands and tossing it aside. "What we are looking for is a map."

"A map to what?"

"The city," he said. "But not exactly. Before Archibald and this sham dragonka fever, the government put a lot of money into building a pneumatic mail delivery system underground. Archibald had it discontinued, and it has since fallen into disrepair. I have been working on fixing it, but to really make use of it, I need to know all the places it reaches. I could just follow where the pipes go, but that could take weeks, and they might lead me to some places that are too risky to explore."

I began to hunt amongst the papers with real purpose. Through reams of dusty, sometimes greasy stacks of wax wrapping, documents, and deeds, we searched. I found a bunch of maps, even ones so old they looked like they should be on a museum wall, but not the exact one Deklyn was looking for. I unfolded one that depicted the city of Pava. Perhaps it was the first time I had seen what Pava looked like from above: the black serpentine river separating the two sides of the city, making Pava look like a giant moth resting on the cold terrain, poised to lift its speckled, sparkling wings and flutter off again at any moment. Or, I reconsidered, like a big broken heart, the bridges like stitching holding it together.

I looked at Deklyn, his black heart tattoo visible through his white blouse. I can't explain the feeling that came over me. It wasn't affection—for I still hated the boy—but I understood that his fate was the fate of Pava. And I loved Pava. He noticed me watching him.

"What?" he said, pausing.

"Nothing," I said. "But what is the Jozseftown Resistance Movement?"

"I can't tell you right now. It is only in its beginning stages. But we are not going to let the Boot dictate what happens here. Jozseftown became world famous from the Dragonka Exchange. And we mean to protect it."

"I can help," I said.

"No," said Deklyn. "It is too dangerous for you. A Pava School girl."

I looked away, feeling resentment burn within me. As if to prove him wrong, I rifled through the papers with more intensity.

Soon curious Kubikula children began to wander into the room, putting their grubby fingers on my clothing, smelling my hair.

"OK," said Deklyn. "Finding the right one was a long shot, anyway. The rumor is that Archibald had ordered them all burned, and the creators of the network exiled."

"What is he so afraid of?"

"Just information. If the JRM can join with other movements against him, it would be a real threat. But as it stands, we are divided. Not to mention, finding an entranceway into the Palace below ground would be invaluable. And I am told the map shows one."

I wanted to hear more, but a Kubikula girl put my finger in her mouth. I screamed, and suddenly more Kubikula children began pouring into the room, attracted by the noise.

"Let's get you out of here before they decide to make a meal of you," he said, perhaps only half joking. We left quickly, a cluster of Kubikula children trailing us into the adjoining sewers, until they were called back by their elders.

We made it away safely, but on our way back to the Blackhearts' lair, I noticed that we were being followed by Sytia. She was running. We stopped and let her catch up with us. She was very excited, carrying a pouch in her hands. We paused to see what she had brought. From the opening she pulled a tiny beast. I could see that it was a dragonka pup. But it had a bizarre coloration, like somebody had dipped it in a murky gold mud. Also, more shockingly, it had long sharp fangs and red eyes, and its forearms appeared stunted and unusable. Stranger still, its wings appeared to be made of metal, and were sutured to its body. It was a terrifying and bizarre-looking beast: half machine, half dragonka.

"Where did you get this?" Deklyn asked the child. She pointed to the dark tunnel. The dragonka had come to her as trash! Deklyn shook his head. "This isn't the first mutation we have seen. Somebody is doing experiments on the dragonka. It looks like they are fashioning them into something bizarre and vicious. They must be discarding their misfires." He handed the mutant beast back to the Kubikula girl.

By the time we arrived back at the Blackheart lair, the others had fallen asleep, and I had to lift my exhausted dragonka from Abel's protective clutch. Deklyn guided me to the entrance of the sewer, where a ladder led me back to the fountain.

Chapter 10

I thought I would be hearing from the Blackhearts soon after that day, but it was actually quite some time before they contacted me again. My absences from home were growing longer and more conspicuous, and now that Luma was training for competitions, he had become more and more rambunctious, flying around my room, scampering from my grasp when I just wanted to pet him out of loneliness. I knew I could not keep Luma a secret from my mother any longer.

As it turned out I didn't have to.

One morning I awoke, and Luma was simply not there. The open cage, and bedroom door—which stood ajar—told the story. Downstairs I could hear mother moving about in the kitchen. I crept quietly down the stairs and peered in the door. What I saw amazed me: mother was holding her palm out and feeding pomegranate seeds to Luma, who was sitting up on his hind legs on the butcher's block. It was the first time in so long that my mother's interest was stirred. She was even laughing a little when the dragonka stuck his tongue out to take the red seeds from her hand. I stood unnoticed at the door, and suddenly felt like I was looking in on a scene from my mother's past, from when before I had been born. My mother even appeared years younger, with a smile spreading across her face, her beauty enthralling even in her night-gown and with hair uncombed. I knew I should not be spying like this, on something that was my mother's private happiness. It was a lonely feeling, but one that also made me brighten inside.

I had been selfish, I realized. I wanted to rush into the kitchen and tell mother that—to confess something, though I was not sure what; no to confess that I had snuck out my window, because I knew that I would continue to commit such misdeeds, but to confess that I was Petra K, that I had always been Petra K and always would be, and I was at once sorry and very proud of that fact. For once it looked like mother would understand. For only a moment I had forgotten completely about the dragonka.

But when I entered in the kitchen, I confessed nothing. I stood by my mother and Luma, continuing to watch, feeling like a small child again. "What should we do?" I asked, not because I wanted advice, but because I wanted mother to know that I thought she was worth asking.

But when she turned to look at me, the entire picture crumpled. My dragonka was one thing, and I was quite another. Her eyes steeled as they pierced me. I shrank back to the door, but mother called me back.

"Petra K," she began. I knew she was angry, because she was whispering. "What have you gotten us into?"

"I had no choice," I began.

"I don't want to hear your excuses!" she spat. I could talk back to anybody, except my mother. Even when I was right, my words just got trapped in my throat, my lips unable to form them, as though I was speaking a foreign language.

"Tell me who you stole it from," she said. "Tell me now."

"I didn't steal it," I said. But the words just fell flat from my mouth. This was one of those times when no matter how true the response, it sounds like a lie, even to your own ears.

"Speak up," Mother said, even though I knew she could hear me well enough.

"I didn't steal it," I said louder.

"You are turning into your father," she shouted.

It was then that my mother grabbed a broom. She struck out at me with it, as though I was a rodent that had gotten indoors. She was not used to moving quickly, so I dodged the bristles easily. I almost wanted to let one blow land, just so she wouldn't feel like such a failure. Instead she took a few more futile swings, then crumpled onto the floor. I approached her silently. I took the broom into my hands, then gently pried it from her grip. She let it go easily. Her hands were so old looking. My heart, as always, filled with pity and love for my mother.

"Come on, it's OK," I said.

"I tried so hard," she said. "I tried so hard to keep you from turning into a deviant. But I failed. I failed terribly."

In such a situation, I knew it was my turn to care for her. That was what both of us expected of me.

"Let's go outside today," I said, forcing a bright smile.

"But I haven't been out in such along time," Mother said.

"I know. That's why it will be great," I answered.

Her demeanor changed in an instant. Anger took too much energy from her. I watched her tense expression relax. From that point on, my mother was like a huge doll I could take charge of. I escorted her into her room, helped her out of her night things, and selected a perfect winter outfit for her. It was perhaps too dressy for just going out to walk around Jozseftown, but that was alright. For me, at least, it was a celebration. She let me comb her hair and put some rouge on her cheeks. There was nothing to be done about the tea-stained teeth, but at least I could count on her not smiling.

When we were done, she looked like I remembered her from before she began locking herself in her bedroom. Which means, great: my mother all over again. I locked Luma in his cage with some water and food, then took Mother by the hand and guided her to the front door. I opened it, and a blast of cold air invaded the hall. We pushed forward and stepped outside. Her head perked up like a flower leaning to sunlight.

I was in no mood for Jozseftown. My mother deserved to see the best of Pava on a day like today. We made our way past the vendors and through the narrow streets, and walked past the guards that stood posted at the neighborhood gates. We strolled across the Karlow Bridge to parade ourselves in our old neighborhood under the Palace.

"Look," Mother said. "The Palace Gardens are open. Let's go see!"

At the gardens we saw rare flowers: kissing tulipan that made a slurping sound as their petals sought each other; orgona from the high Nepyls, which gave off the odor of bitter chocolate and whose petals were prized by top pastry chefs; and the dark violet *lavendula*, the touch of which causes an instant and deep sleep. As we strolled, we passed uniformed generals, ministers, and their families, and troops of gardeners who tried to make themselves invisible whenever anybody important approached.

"My heavens," Mother exclaimed, grabbing me by the shoulder.

"Ouch!" I exclaimed back.

"There he is, stand aside. Curtsy. Do anything, just don't misbehave!"

I saw at once whom she was talking about. A short person was walking toward us, his nose held high in the air. As he approached, we tried to flatten ourselves against the side of the path. It was Archibald the Precious himself, two Boot minders walking behind him. Every now and again one of the Boot guards would point out a particularly spectacular flower and bend it toward Archibald to smell, at which point Archibald would pluck the flower from its stem and hand it back to a guard, whose job it was to carry the bouquet. It was funny to see such huge men taking care over such a small delicate thing as a flower.

Soon, though, Archibald was right in front of us. I could see my mother shrinking from his gaze, trying to figure out if she should move left or right. But Archibald just stepped between my mother and me, parting us without a word. You see, behind us was a uniquely huge lavender orchid, with a blossom so big and inviting you could stick your whole face into its cupped petals. And that is just what Archibald did. I could have extended my hand and pet him on the top of his head as he bent toward the flower. He picked the flower himself, then after straightening up he held the orchid out to me, his face brightening as though in recognition. He was about to speak, then something surprising happened: he keeled over and fell flat onto the dirt. For a moment I saw him not as a dictator or enemy, but rather as a classmate who was playacting.

"Oh get up," I said. I could see him taking deep breaths. But Archibald did not get up, and in a split second the Boot were pushing us out of the way. One bent over and lifted Archibald from the ground, then rushed off with the limp body. The other looked around, as though trying to pinpoint a perpetrator.

"You two," he said to us. "Stay right here. Under order of the Boot, do not move from this spot," he commanded, and then rushed after the other Boot guard. My mother looked petrified.

"Come on, Mother," I said, taking her hand. "Let's go!"

"He said to stay here," she responded meekly.

"Yes, but we should really leave," I said.

"You need to learn to do what you are told, Petra K. Who put the idea in your head that you can defy a Boot officer?"

I didn't know how, but I had to get myself and my mother out of there. From where I was standing I could see a commotion at the entrance of the gardens. Boot officers were gathering, and I could see them pulling people from the crowd and leading them away.

"This way," a voice bellowed from behind us. I felt a hand on my shoulder. I turned to say something, to make any excuse I could think of, but there in front of me was Abel, dressed in a Youth Guard uniform. He winked at me, and told us to follow him. I was so surprised that I could not move for a moment.

"This way," he commanded again, though I could see he was also trying to keep from laughing.

"Come, Petra K," my mother instructed, grabbing my hand. We both followed Abel out of the gardens, right under the eye of the Boot. Nobody even looked at us twice.

At once I felt relieved and worried. Why would my mother go with somebody, just because they wore a uniform? Abel was smaller than me, and not terribly convincing as a Youth Guard member. Was it a kind of subtle magic that people want to be deceived by, this complacence in the face of a uniform?

"OK, you are free to go!" Abel said with mock authority, once he had led us to the head of Karlow Bridge.

"But don't you want to question us?" asked my mother.

"Yes," said Abel, a mischievous glimmer rising in his eye. "Questioning. Where do you come from?"

"Jozseftown," she responded dutifully.

"Do you like it there?"

"Not very much," she said honestly.

"And do you like rabbits?" he said, as sternly as possible.

"Why, yes, I suppose. . . ." she stammered.

"Do you own any rabbits, madam?"

"No," she said, still following his lead.

"Not even a small one? I find that a little bunny," Abel said, laughing at his own stupid pun. I wanted to kick him.

"I don't understand what this has to do with what just happened in the Palace Gardens," she said. "We were right there. We didn't do anything, he just fell over in front of us."

"You know," Abel said, trying to be serious, "Archibald has become quite sick. Nobody knows the source of his illness, but we are taking it very seriously, and thank you for your attention."

"You are quite welcome," my mother responded. At last, now we could leave. We began to walk away. But suddenly Abel called us back.

"Ladies, I insist you make haste in getting home, and don't talk to anybody about what you saw."

"We won't, will we Petra K?"

"No," I said.

"Can I talk with the little girl for a moment?" Abel said.

"Of course," my mother said, pushing me in his direction.

"You are littler than me!" I hissed, out of Mother's earshot.

"Friday, be prepared," he said to me in a whisper, then turned and left, disappearing into the crowd that was gathering around the gardens.

"What was that?" said my mother. "I don't understand. How do you know that person?"

"I don't," I lied.

"Then why did he say, Friday? I heard him say *Friday* from here."

"He said that if I ever get a rabbit to name it Friday," I said, mentally lashing Abel for his indiscretion. On the other hand, he did save us from the Boot, as though it was nothing but a game of charades to him.

"Let's get home," Mother said. "It's what we were instructed to do. And he may be a Boot officer, but don't think that you are getting a rabbit too."

We walked in silence back to Jozseftown. When we arrived home, mother went straight to her room, closing the door quietly behind herself, secluded again. She would not emerge again for quite some time.

As it turned out, I would see the Blackhearts before Friday. My mother, I could see, had submitted to a kind of forfeit, though there had been no actual battle. Now I had the run of the house, and Luma and I took full advantage of it. We did raucous exercises on the stairwell, splurged on delicacies from the black market: now that Luma was a champion he was developing an appetite for finer foods. I stopped short of buying him a tin of Kaspian caviar, instead opting for cheaper roe of carp from the Pava River. I knew in my heart that we were behaving badly—people were struggling to just feed themselves in my own neighborhood; but for once I was able to indulge myself, and I was going to do it, all the while without a peep coming from behind mother's door.

The chaos inside my house was only matched by the tense quiet on the streets outside. Boot incursions into the neighborhood were becoming more and more frequent. A man was flogged on Goat Square when it was discovered he had not surrendered his gold tooth; dragonka pups were captured from secret hatcheries. More worrisome, notices were tacked to the lampposts offering a thousand kuna for the deliverance of any dragonka to the Boot Guard, provided the beast was alive and not over a year old. What the Palace wanted with the dragonka was still a mystery to me. All the same, I would have to be doubly sure to keep Luma under wraps and at home.

I wanted to hear what the people of the neighborhood were saying about Archibald at the market, but with no school to attend I had begun to wake up later and later. The shopkeepers were notorious early risers, and were usually done with their trade by early afternoon, but that day I was just in time to catch a few of the last stragglers. I wove in and out of stout women's legs, hanging around quietly until I heard Archibald's name.

"They say he is quite sick," said one woman, handing a few kuna to a vendor selling onions and turnips.

"Who is 'they'?" said another.

"The same they as last time," joked the woman. "Just *they*."

"Only an operation can save him, but nobody dares try," chimed in another.

"It is an issue of the heart," said the grocer. "His heart is bad."

"Bad?" said the young mother. "Try rotten through and through!"

"Shhh, shhh, now," said the older woman when she noticed I was listening in. It was funny to be taken for a spy. A mischievous spirit overtook me, and just to make them nervous I took a pen and piece of paper from my bag and began to write.

"Oh!" exclaimed the grocer. "That's just Petra K. Pay no mind to her. Jozsef K's daughter, you know."

"My," cooed the older woman. My father had a reputation indeed. "Come here, child, and let me look at you. Daughter of the Thief of Hearts."

But nothing made me more nervous than old-woman hands, so I backed away.

"And to think we were afraid of her," added the young mother. "She has the blood of Pava's greatest criminal running in her veins." That's the problem with information, sometimes you just want a sip, but a whole wave comes splashing down on your head. Then, instantaneously, my attention was drawn elsewhere. Across the square, I was sure I spotted Zsofia. I had not seen her since that night outside my window, a few weeks ago. Now was my chance to catch up with her.

I started after Zsofia quickly, but in no time she was lost in the crowd. I searched and searched until I saw her disappearing around a corner into a causeway that led away from Goat Square. I had lost her once on her mysterious late-night jaunt through Jozseftown, and I wasn't about to let it happen again. I followed her, but she was rushing, so it was all I could do to keep her in the distance ahead. I called out to her, but in an instant she expertly scaled the wall that enclosed the Jozseftown cemetery. I saw that she had used a tendril of ivy to help her over, so I took a deep breath and started after her.

I looked around the famous Zsida cemetery from my place high on the wall. The graves were packed so close to each other that the gravestones fanned out from the ground like a hand of sloppily held cards. Notes to the dead, kept in place by silver coins, were balanced on the tops of some of the stones—even in these destitute times people still offered the coins—such was the strength of superstition in Jozseftown.

After I jumped down onto the other side I began to doubt my wisdom in coming here. The place felt unnatural, and there was a fine mist forming in the air, seemingly coming from no-where. There was no sign of Zsofia, but I could sense that she was here. I walked in between the gravestones, rounded crypts, and mausoleums, trying to spot her. It was totally dark by now, though the mist gave off an eerie green glow. I called out her name. The only response was the call of a raven that sat on a gravestone watching me quizzically.

There, from behind the door of a mausoleum ahead of me, came a glow. I approached on silent feet, dashing from tomb to tomb for cover. Once I was close, I peered around the stone. From where I hid I could see a shadow passing in front of the light, and heard a rustling coming from inside the mausoleum. I crept to the door quietly and pressed my head to where it was cracked open. The place was empty. Where had Zsofia gone? I pushed back the door and entered. After a thorough search I concluded that there was no other exit. But she had to have been here: I could smell, hanging faintly in the air, the black vial perfume from Ludmilla's.

Chapter 11

That night came the dreams of gnashing fangs, of an invisible, formless evil chasing me in the fog: a shared nightmare with Luma, who shuddered beside me. I awoke, sitting bolt upright in bed. *Somebody was watching me as I slept.* A hooded figure hovered there, outside my window. Wormwood had followed me, he had come to take Luma. The window frame rattled as it was jarred loose, and before I had time to react, the window was thrown open and the figure tumbled into my room.

"You should lock your window at night," said Abel.

"What are you doing here?" I said.

"There was a change of plans," he answered.

"What do you mean?" I asked, rubbing my eyes.

"Hey! A frog!" he said, picking up one of my stuffed animals and making a croaking sound. "Wow, you've really got everything."

"Quiet, you'll wake my mom," I said.

"Somebody should," he replied snidely. "Sleepwalking around the Palace is not safe." I knew Abel was right, but still I didn't like anybody criticizing my mother but me.

"Enough. Now what change of plans are you talking about?"

"The tournament. It has been moved."

"What tournament? Where?"

"The *next* tournament. It's outside the city now," he whispered. "It has become too risky to stage them at the old Exchange. Boot guards are coming and going at all hours these days, and several dragonka were even turned in to them by their owners."

"So where is the next Maiden and Minor Pup?"

"In a town near the Lower Tatras," he said.

"But I can't travel that far from home," I said. "I need to take care of my mother."

"Then you will have to give Luma to us for the night," Abel responded.

I considered this for a moment. If I wanted to continue earning our keep through Luma, I felt I would have to agree.

"How do I know you will bring him back?" I said.

"Do you think I would have saved you from the Boot in the Palace Gardens if I planned on stealing Luma?" said Abel. "Look, nobody will tell you this, but Luma is not the same when you are not around. He pouts like his world is doomed, doesn't let Isobel apply the sparkles, and he even nipped my finger when I tried to feed him some pomegranate seeds."

I could not conceal my pleasure on hearing this, and a smile broke out across my face.

"Don't laugh," said Abel. "It hurt."

"I'm not laughing," I said.

"Yeah, right," said Abel, who began to investigate my room.

"So we agree," I said.

"Sure," replied Abel blithely.

"So you should leave," I said.

"Oh," rejoined Abel. "The only thing is, I need to take Luma tonight. The tournament is tomorrow."

"What? Why are you telling me now?"

Abel just shrugged, and kept playing with the stuffed frog.

When I went to wake Luma, he protested fiercely, spitting at us through the bars of his cage. "You shouldn't surprise us like this," I said to Abel. "I'm going to have to take him as far as your lair. You can give him some lavendula to calm him for the trip."

"Why don't you just come with us?" said Abel.

I thought about my mother, how she would react if I just disappeared, or if she would react at all.

"I can't," I said. "I have a home, Abel." His face momentarily fell. That was the real difference between us, not the stuffed frogs or schooling: I had a home, something Abel might never know.

"Fine," he finally responded. "Just get him as far as the lair." Then he put the frog down, went to the window, and slipped out, silent as a breeze. I thought for a second, feeling bad without any real reason to. I opened Luma's cage and pulled him out. I stroked him until he was calm, put on my jacket, and tucked him and the portable nest into the inner pocket. I started out the window, then thought of something. I pulled myself back inside, then went and grabbed the stuffed frog.

"Hey Abel," I called out my window. When he looked up, I tossed the frog out. He caught it, and couldn't contain the smile it brought to his face. After that, I slipped from the window and joined him on the dark Jozseftown street.

Luma sensed our impending separation and it was all I could do to keep him from escaping from my coat. Dawn was breaking in the neighborhood: I could even see a few stalls being set up on Goat Square Market. There was a kind of silence on the streets, a silence that spoke, like a hot wind before a thunderstorm. Something was about to happen, this was clear to me. Oblivious, the rest of the city carried on as normal: street sweepers brushed the dust and trash from the gutters, and revelers sang drunkenly on their way home from long nights at the pubs. On the corner, an automaton creaked awake, a light glowing from behind its glass eye, seeking customers. An old beggar man stopped us to ask for alms. Abel handed over a few kuna. The thousand kuna that the Boot were offering would buy a lot of meals. I wondered just how many of these people would turn in Luma and me for the sake of that money.

Before long we came to the metal grate and descended into the sewers. Deklyn and Isobel were there, awake and ready to travel. I set Luma down on the table. He looked about anxiously, until Isobel fed him a petal of lavendula that she had produced from a vial. He took it greedily from her fingertips, and before long was snoozing on the card table.

"When will you be back?" I asked.

"It depends on Luma, but if he wins, not until tomorrow night."

Something wasn't right. Nobody was speaking much, or looking me in the eye.

"What's wrong?" I said.

"Nothing," Abel was quick to answer.

"Yes, there is," I insisted.

"Jasper was arrested near the palace," Deklyn finally said. "He was trying to make contact with the other resistance movements."

"What?" shrieked Abel.

"We just heard. Anyway, we have to move now. There is no time to waste. Petra K, it is time for you to leave. We have to plan."

"Come," said Isobel, taking me by the hand. "Deklyn needs to be alone right now."

"But he is not alone," I protested. "Even if I leave, he is not alone."

"It is better if you get home right now. It is not safe here."

In a daze, I let Isobel take me by the arm and escort me out. I found myself on the street. I began to walk home with a bad feeling in my stomach. Something was happening that I was not being told about, something more than Jasper. I was suddenly unsure if I could fully trust the Blackhearts.

In my path stood an old Half Not woman. I could see that she was blind, but she sensed me all the same, and beckoned me forward to read my fortune. Half Nots were famous for the accuracy of their fortunetelling, so I complied, taking a kuna from my pocket and placing it in her grimy hand. After I did that she began to run her fingers over my own palm, tracing the lines of my hand. "Ahhh," she moaned, her eyes rolling back into her head. "Mists of the night clearing! River clay molding itself! Betrayal is at hand! And it comes from one so close to you! You are in great danger. The time is now, you must act." With that, the Half Not dropped my hand, her eyes becoming lucid for a moment. I would swear she could see, for she put her hand to my face and whispered, "So much depends upon it, Petra K."

She knew my name! I knew right then that I had been betrayed by the Blackhearts. After the tournament, they were going to turn Luma in to the Boot and claim the money. I rushed back to the grate, lifted it, and descended into the sewer. I ran along the dark old passageways until I got to their lair.

I was too late. The place was empty. Barely a trace of the Blackhearts remained, just a few blankets and vials of useless potion. Jasper's model of Ruki Mur was gone as well, though a few spare limbs lay discarded in the corner. The gang had instantly vanished.

I would have to catch up with them. This meant somehow getting to the Lower Tatras. Could I actually do something like that? I had never taken a train by myself, and only been out of the city on a few trips with my mother to pick apples.

I returned home, throwing open the front door rather than climbing up the ivy. But when I entered the foyer, I was greeted by two uniformed Boot officers and a man in a white lab coat.

"That's her," said the doctor. One of the Boot officers moved quickly to block my escape. The other closed in on me. I made a start toward the door but was grabbed from behind. He held me firmly by my arms, and struggle as I might, I could not escape. The doctor approached. He put the back of his hand to my forehead, then looked me closely in the eyes.

"Yes," he said. "A case of dragonka fever in its incubation. But don't worry, child, we will take care of you." It was then that I noticed: in his other hand he held a dragon-headed staff. I registered the deathly astringent smell of camphor. It was Wormwood. He was not a trader at all, but an agent of the Boot.

Before they took me, I saw the door to mother's bedroom open but a crack. I saw a shape darken that space, and then I saw it close. I called out to her—the woman who had betrayed me, the woman who had turned me over to the Boot. I was dragged from the house, without a peep from Katalin K.

Chapter 12

In a Boot cart I was taken on a familiar route: to the Pava School. Only now, from the building's main entrance hall hung two long red and black banners, with Archibald's Imperial symbol—a golden eye—peering out from it, as though gazing across the domain of the schoolyard. I saw two more Imperial insignias where the Pava School sign once was. Only now it read "Pava Youth Guard Facility." Gone were the peacocks, and the flower gardens had been torn up, replaced by statues of Archibald. The guard escorted me into the building. With one whiff, memories of school came rushing back. They could change the name and hang posters of Archibald up and down the hallways, but the place still smelled like my old school.

As we passed one of the classrooms, I peered in. There were all my old classmates, minus Zsofia, concentrating on the lesson, delivered by a uniformed teacher.

"That is not for you," said my escort. "Not yet. The Number One Play Pal's teachings are still beyond you."

There it was again, that silly name people had invented for the dictator. "Why don't you just call him Archibald?" I said.

"Some do," the escort answered. "But that is just one aspect of him. Here, he is Number One Play Pal. It is something of a nickname, because you are blessed with the advantage of enjoying the great fun our leader has to offer. You will realize there is no better playmate than our leader."

We arrived at a basement room, the door was opened, and I was pushed into darkness.

"Quarantine," the guard said, and then she locked the door and left me there, alone. I could not see an inch ahead of me, so I felt with my hands until I found a mattress on the floor. There I sat and waited. But nobody came. So I waited more. And more.

And still more.

THERE IS NO SUCH THING as darkness. That is what I came to realize. If you are put in a blackened cell for hours, days at a time, you create your own light. Where it comes from I don't know, perhaps the tiny part of your mind where hope still shines. But there in front of me was Luma again, in a waking dream, frolicking in the air with his strange cursive flying. He was alive; he was well. I could feel it in my heart. I knew then that the Blackhearts had not betrayed me. It was my mother and my mother alone whom the Half Not fortuneteller had spoken of. Had my mother told them about my pet, or had she simply gotten rid of me like a houseplant that had outgrown its space? For that answer I would have to wait. And wait I did. I have no idea how long, because without the sun the days smeared into the night, night smudged into day, the whole thing a dark murky painting of time. But why did I feel no hunger? There had to be a reason for the madness, unless it was just for the sake of madness.

The more I stayed alone, the stronger I felt Luma's presence. Perhaps Isobel's exercises really bonded us, and we inhabited a part of each other's hearts. Perhaps that is what Isobel meant by the magic coming from inside. For the beast could be nothing but a projection of my enfeebled mind. Or perhaps I was just going loony from the isolation. But Luma was conjured again before my eyes, sparkling in the darkness. I grabbed the phantom beast, and we did a dance together, moving clumsily across the room. Then Luma crumbled from my grasp, disappearing like a sand castle in the rain. I called his name, but got no response.

Then I cried.

When I had no more tears, I crawled to the mattress again to try to sleep. I lay down my head on the musty pillow. I let my eyelids slowly close; upon doing so I heard a whirring, clapping sound. There was a bird in my cell! And it was circling around my face, like a hummingbird hovers in front of a flower. It stayed there for a few moments, then rose again to its roost somewhere in the blackness above me. Again I closed my eyes to sleep, and again the bird descended. Again I opened my eyes. After it happened a third time, I began to get annoyed. It seemed to come and flutter right in my face right when my eyes closed, as though it was there to keep me from sleeping. When it happened again, I clinched my eyes shut tight. This time the bird fluttered down, and flew around my face, but I would not open my eyes. I swiped at it with my hand to lightly knock it away, but when I touched it I felt not feathers but fur. Rather than a bird, it was a huge bat, there in the room with me. I shot upright and screamed. I heard the bat hit the wall, recover from my swat, then return to its place above. I didn't close my eyes again for a very long time.

I HAVE NO IDEA HOW LONG I lived in that waking sleep—it must have been days—but just when I thought I could bear it no more, when I was surviving as but a husk of myself, I heard sounds coming from outside the door. Voices resounded high and excited. Girls were singing and laughing.

The door burst open, and even though the light in the corridor was dim, I still had to shield my eyes against it. I immediately felt hands upon me, stroking my hair, patting my back. Then somebody hugged me.

"Welcome. Now, let's get down to play." Though my eyes were closed against the light, I recognized the voice. It was Bianka and my old classmates: Lenka, Margo, and Sonia. Only Tatiana was missing. It had been so long since I had had any human contact. Their hands felt warm and pleasing when they brushed me. I fell into their arms and let them ply me like a piece of clay from the Pava riverbed. When I was able to open my eyes again, I saw their faces. They somehow looked older, and harder, and they all wore the same black pajamas with a red sash. I looked up and could not believe the size of the bat I was sharing a room with. It was as big as a hawk, and had crimson red fur. The monstrous creature stared down at me with tiny black eyes.

"You met Lapis," said Bianka of the bat.

"Yes," I answered meekly.

"Come here, Lapis," Bianka commanded. The bat glided down to her shoulder like a trained falcon. "Lapis keeps us on our toes when our attention strays."

"Let's go," she said. "The others are waiting."

"The others?"

"Yeah," said Margo. "It is your birthday night!"

"But it's not my birthday yet!" I said. It wasn't possible I had been kept in that room throughout the whole winter.

"Yes it is," countered Sonia. "You are reborn today. You are a brand new person." And with no further delay they took me by my hands and led me along the darkened hallway of my old school. I knew it was evening because no light came from the windows. The walls were festooned with crepe-paper flowers and portraits of Archibald the Precious. Lapis flew alongside us as we walked. The girls sang a quiet song that I had never heard before; they all knew the lyrics and looked back and forth between one another, as though the song brought on great memories for them. Everybody just seemed so happy; it made me feel strange and kind of bad for being suspicious of them.

We arrived at what was the old science classroom. There, candles had been lit and incense burned in pots. A chair—no—something more like a throne, sat in the center of the room. To this seat I was brought. I sat down and the group joined hands around me, singing their strange song. Then the equipment-room door was thrust open, and from it marched Tatiana. In her hands she carried a wrapped package. As she approached, a smile broke out on her face. The room had gone silent, my classmates prickling in anticipation. Tatiana held the box out to me.

"Happy Birthday," she said warmly as I accepted the gift. Everybody went quiet as I opened the box. Inside I found a black shirt and pants—a uniform of the Boot Youth Guard, along with an armband with a guard insignia: a golden sun.

"You will get your official Youth Guard pin after initiation," Tatiana informed me. "Now try on the uniform." I changed into the black slacks and stiff-collared shirt. They were a little big, and felt a bit like wearing pajamas.

"Perfect," said Margo, ignoring the poor fit. I became self-conscious because everybody was gazing at me with adoring, if not expectant eyes. I was exhausted and had no idea what was expected of me. Should I salute? Fortunately, the moment did not last too long. I noticed that a few of the girls' eyes began to droop. Lapis quickly descended from the ceiling and flapped his wings in their faces, giving each a firm slap. Alert again, they reoriented themselves, then carried on as if nothing had happened.

"Playtime!" Sonia shouted from nowhere.

"Playtime," the others resounded in chorus. "Quick, we will be late." And, with that, they hustled me off to another classroom. To my amazement, there was Miss Kavanova, standing at the chalkboard, also dressed in a Boot uniform. She too looked like she suffered from lack of sleep, her dark eyes peering out like pits in a prune. If she recognized me, she gave no hint of it.

"It's me, Miss Kavanova, Petra K," I said.

The class erupted in a nervous laughter. She calmed them with a stern look. "It's OK," she said. "You were like that as newborns as well."

"My name," she said to me, "is Agent One O' Clock."

"It is Miss Kavanova," I countered. "We already know each other." I should have kept my mouth shut. This time the class didn't giggle, but went quiet instead. Miss Kavanova approached me, and as she did the room appeared to darken, or maybe it was just my sudden fear that I had made a terrible mistake. She stood over me, then cracked the ruler down on my desk. "Count off, class!"

"Youth Guard Agent One Ten," yelled Margo, standing up straight.

"Youth Guard Agent One Twenty," yelled Sonia. And so it went, each one calling out their names.

"I am the hour One O' Clock," repeated Miss Kavanova. "And you are all my minutes."

"What minute will she be?" Tatiana called out.

"Well," considered Miss Kavanova, "I think we should name her One Fifty. Then we have an hour."

"Yeah," the class cheered.

"One Fifty it is," said Miss Kavanova. "Circle around me." The class did so, like numerals on a clock. I saw my place at the fifty-minute mark, and took it.

"Lucky class," Miss Kavanova said. "Today we will show our birthday girl a presentation." The class broke out in excited whispers. "Yes," said Miss Kavanova. "Prepare! You know what to do! It is the story of Monarch Trymosyn and the Twelve Alchemists!" No sooner had she spoken than Tatiana and Sonia ran to the back of the classroom and pulled a small puppet stage to the front of the class. Others busied themselves behind the stage, giggling in excitement. The curtains of the room were drawn and a candle was lit.

"Now, Agent One Fifty, pay close attention," instructed Miss Kavanova. A marionette dressed in the old costume of a Pava commoner dropped onto the stage. All eyes were trained on the puppet narrator.

Trymosyn and the Twelve Alchemists

NARRATOR: Trymosyn, thirteenth monarch of Dravonia, who ruled over a century ago, was a monarch of great wealth, but like those with much money, he only wanted more. So he used his influence to gather the twelve most renowned alchemists—which is a person who makes gold from lead, for those of you who don't know—from across the world, and built vast laboratories beneath the Palace to house them and their studies. Now, alchemists, introduce yourselves!

Dropping onto the stage, ALCHEMIST # 1: Nester Nersessian!

ALCHEMIST # 2: Ogilvya of Mangolvya!

ALCHEMIST # 3: Count Brohumil!

ALCHEMIST # 4: Momotoro of Greater Kori!

(And so it went until there were twelve marionettes on the stage plus Monarch Trymosyn, each costumed in colorful dress from their native lands.)

NARRATOR: They were given anything they wished for and worked around the clock in pursuit of their desire: gold. Some experimented with necromancy, the art of raising the dead, to extract their secrets.

ALCHEMIST # 1 *(standing over a marionette corpse)* Rise! *(A puff of smoke, and the corpse rose, then ran off the stage.)*

NARRATOR: Others were charlatans, with no real scientific knowledge whatsoever, except how to spend the monarch's money.

ALCHEMESTS # 5, 6, 7 & 8 (*sitting around a card table, playing hands of cards*)

NARRATOR: But none actually made progress toward achieving their end of fashioning gold from nothing.

ALCHEMIST #3: Eureka! (*a puff of smoke, a flash of black*) *ALCHEMISTS #4 and 5 look on, shaking their heads in disapproval.*

NARRATOR: When the monarch came to check on their work, they all pretended everything was fine. The alchemists only wanted to continue their work, so sometimes they sated the monarch's greed with fool's gold, or refused to let him into the laboratory. But as their experiments failed to yield real results, the king lost interest in them. Instead, he funded the Breeders Guild, who were having great success in dragonka breeding. (*A dragonka marionette now dropped onto the stage, at which point the class booed.*) The monarch, bored with his alchemists, had them bricked into their laboratories, where it was thought they died lonely painful deaths.

(The ALCHEMISTS *die dramatically.*) Or did they? All that dark magic has had an effect, and the spirits of the alchemists were trapped in the Palace. Henceforth they became known as *Haints*—spirits that still have a hold on the material world. In this form, they continued doing the king's bidding, making fantastic strides in their craft. Though for this they need gold, because gold is light, and light keeps them in this world.

(*All alchemists awaken, and extend their hands.*)

ALCHEMISTS: Gold! Give us gold! *(Golden coins rain down on them—and the Alchemists rejoice.)*

NARRATOR: It is our job to honor them, for the alchemists died in service of the king. Even in spirit form, they continue their work, creating gold from nothing at all. This has been a presentation approved by The Ministry of Unlikely Occurrences.

THE END

THE STAGE WENT DARK, and the class roared its approval, and Miss Kavanova threw a handful of fool's gold coins at the stage like a tip. Tatiana and the other players came from behind the stage to receive applause.

"Is all that true?" I whispered to Bianka.

"Of course," she said. "Unless it is not. The only important thing is that Number One Play Pal wants us to honor the memory of the alchemists. As we should."

THAT NIGHT WAS THE FIRST TIME I was allowed to sleep. We were all bunking together in beds set up in a former classroom. I don't know how long I had been dozing, but it couldn't have been for more than a few hours when I was awoken abruptly by somebody shaking me. It was Bianka.

"You were calling out in your sleep!" she said. I immediately stiffened. What had I said?

"Katalin K is fine. Everybody has dreams like that at first. You will forget in time. It happened to all of us."

"Where are your parents?" I asked.

"I have no parents," she responded automatically. "I am but a minute in the hour. The hours belong to Archibald. He is our day and night." She must have seen the apprehension in my face, because she continued.

"The people who raised me are in the marshes somewhere in the south. I have not seen them since the Ministry of Unlikely Occurrences saved me from the dragonka fever. But time moves forward, not backward, so I do my best to forget about them." I could see Bianka feared even mentioning her parents: she had looked around to make sure nobody was listening before uttering that statement. I too followed her gaze. But something was amiss. The room was empty. Where there had been six full beds when I lay down, there were now five empty ones.

"Where is everybody?"

"That's actually why I woke you. To come and get you," she said.

"For what?"

"For the *real* play," she responded, her eyes widening.

"I want to go home," I said. "I don't want to play."

"You won't make it past the gate," she answered. "Think of this as your home from now on."

"I can't," I said quietly.

"Petra K," she said, using my real name. It was the first time anybody had done so since I was taken away. "If you don't want to play, then *play along*. That's all I am going to say." I got the message: not everyone was as obedient as they appeared in the Youth Guard Facility. I dressed in my starchy uniform and accompanied Bianka out of the room and down the hallway. We arrived at the gymnasium, where she turned the door handle and slowly opened the door. We tiptoed in. In the middle of the room were the rest of the girls. They stood in a circle, just like they had been in class, only now there was somebody other than Miss Kavanova in the center.

It took me but a moment to realize it was Jasper, tied to a chair.

Chapter 13

I didn't know what to do. Jasper was undergoing some kind of torture. The girls each wore long robes and held daggers, which they were waving in front of Jasper's face. "*Play along*," repeated Bianka, whispering in my ear. "For his sake. For everybody's." It was then that I noticed, in the back of the gym, flickering in and out of the darkness, the shaded shapes of figures, observing the exercise. I could barely make them out; they were like oily slicks against dark waters.

We joined the circle in our corresponding places. Nobody glanced at us—we were expected. Suddenly Jasper's eyes caught mine; they widened in recognition, but he wisely kept his mouth shut. I imagine he thought I was his only hope. It relaxed him, for some reason. He stopped struggling against the ties that bound him. When this happened, Tatiana approached Jasper from behind. She covered his mouth with a handkerchief, which must have contained a sleeping agent, because he passed out within seconds. Tatiana patted his forehead, as though in affection. I had no idea what was going on, but there was no way I could have been prepared for what happened next. Sonia stepped forward. In her hands was the mask of some strange animal. She slipped it over the boy's head. It was then that I realized it was a dragonka mask, made of wood and painted with blazing green and yellow, with sticks sharpened to spike like fangs, tipped by drops of red blood.

Tatiana, meanwhile, was undoing his ties. When she finished, she rejoined the circle. Soon, Jasper began to twitch, as though lost in a terrible dream.

"Rise," Tatiana commanded. Jasper twitched with greater agitation, then lifted himself shakily from his chair. The dragonka mask made him look like some sort of monster. From a side room, a new boy was led into the gymnasium by another troop of Youth Guard, some of whom I recognized from the upper grades at the Pava School.

"Are you ready to play?" the senior representative of the other troop asked Tatiana.

"Yes," she responded.

"Then let's begin the heart-to-heart."

Pylons were set up around the room, and when the leader of the other troop counted down from five, the other boy entered the ring. With a jab from Tatiana's finger, Jasper was pushed into the ring as well. I could see now that it was meant to be some sort of fight. The other boy, who wore a bright red dragonka mask, approached Jasper, his arms outstretched like a monkey about to beat its chest. He grabbed Jasper by the shoulders and tried to throw him to the ground. Jasper, who appeared fully awake now, resisted. He attacked back, and soon they were rolling around the ring, trying to wrestle each other into submission. All the spectators cheered them on, making imaginary bets. I could not help notice how similar our game was to the dragonka competition, except we were playing with people.

They fought fiercely, throwing one another to the ground, pounding each other with their fists. They paused between bouts, panting, rubbing their sores. But, in the end, Jasper overcame the other boy. The beaten child lay still on the floor. A chant began to rise from the audience. "Play! Play! Play!" they yelled. Tatiana came into the ring and presented Jasper with a long bone-white dagger. She then pointed to the heart of the other boy. Without pausing, Jasper raised the knife.

"Stop!" I screamed.

Everybody turned to face me. It was quiet as a graveyard, until Jasper dropped the knife. I opened my mouth to say something. Tatiana just looked at me, shaking her head. A rustling sound came from the back of the room: the shadowy figures were moving about frantically. I turned and ran from that place. As I ran down the corridor, I could hear the flapping wings of Lapis behind me. I tried to outrun him, but it was not possible—he shadowed me from a short distance over my head. I burst through the school door, and made my way through the gardens. I stumbled over bushes and roots, seeking the wrought iron fence, which I knew I could scale. All the while, Lapis flew stealthily above. I saw the fence ahead, but right before I reached it, a cloaked shape rose in front of me, like a dark spirit rising from a grave. It was one of the figures that had been hovering in the dark of the gymnasium. It had followed me, and indeed gotten ahead of me. I jumped for the fence, but before my hands found the top, the shadow captured me and folded me in its foggy arms, and like a butterfly that had been netted and etherized, I was instantly lost in blackness and the smell of camphor. I fell into unconsciousness. I remember nothing more from that night.

Chapter 14

Again I awoke back in my darkened cell in the Dream Chamber. I had to get out of that room. I screamed and kicked against the door, but it would not budge. I felt along the wall for a crack I could chip away at, but there was none. The only sound was that of Lapis quietly panting above me. Again, I hit the door as hard as I could. After I realized I was helpless, I quietly withdrew into myself again. I prayed only for light and company. Any company but that of Lapis, who maintained his vigil above me—keeping me awake. How I regretted running loose from my mother's control.

MUCH LATER, I finally heard the telltale sound of footsteps approaching from the hall. They stopped outside the Dream Chamber. The door opened slowly, and I cowered in the corner. But when I saw who it was, I sprang from my place: there was my mother. She was dressed up again, wearing a sleek black jacket; her hair was smartly trimmed. She held me to her as never before.

Then she put her face up to mine and brushed the small tears from my cheeks.

"Everything will be alright," she said. "I love you, Petra K."

"I want to go home," I said.

"This is home from now on," she said.

"No!" I said.

"I can't stay long," she said. "Tell me, Petrushka, where is Luma now?"

"I don't know," I said honestly.

"Don't be like that," she said. My mother was never a convincing liar, and now I detected something false in her voice. "The sooner all of those beasts are off the street, the sooner we can be together again."

"But what do they want with the dragonka? What does it even matter?"

"It is for their protection. Terrible things are happening to them."

"What?"

"I don't want to tell you. Oh, Petrushka, these child gangs are selling them abroad. People are making handbags out of them. Shoes, wallets, whatever you want."

"That's not true," I said.

"It is, and if you had believed me from the start about them, you never would have been in this mess," she said. "Everything is being done for their protection—and yours." I hung down my head and closed my eyes in thought. I have to confess that my suspicions about the Blackhearts crept back in. Why did they take Luma away? Where was he now? How I missed my mother, and how I would love to boil a pot for her tea again. But wait—wasn't she right here? How did I miss her if she was right here with me? I looked up again, but there was nobody. Where had she gone? The door was closed, but I had not heard her leave. Was it possible that she was not in the Dream Chamber at all? That I was only imagining her?

It was then I realized that—like magic—the nightmares of the Dream Chamber came from me and nobody else. What I experienced is what I brought in with me. With that thought, I began to empty my mind. I tried to erase the memory of the shy Petra K who was afraid of her classmates; I banished my angry mother from my mind as well. Her place was at home, not here with me.

Something cracked in me, all my emotion and self-pity and grief spilled out in that dark room. The tears were simply the still water drawn from the bottom of a very deep well. After I was finished, there was nothing left inside. I was an empty space waiting to be filled.

Before long, footsteps sounded outside the door again. The small figure of Bianka stood in the opened frame.

"Are you OK?" she asked.

"Yes," I said. "I am ready to play." But what I really meant was, "I am ready to *play along.*"

IN CLASS AGAIN, Miss Kavanova held up a wallet for display, then a handbag, and then a belt.

"Pure well-tanned dragonka leather," she said, leveling her gaze at me. "Available at any Kina shop abroad."

"Where did you get that?" Bianka gasped.

"It is not important," she said. "But if you are willing to pay, you can even get them in Pava, on the black market."

"But how can they do that?" I asked, standing, feeling outrage rise within me.

Miss Kavanova smiled, and walked over to me. She placed her hand on my shoulder. For the first time, she felt like my old teacher.

"Don't blame them too much," she said. "They have not had an education like you. What they need is protection. Protection from themselves. That is what the Number One Play Pal offers. Isn't that right, Margo?"

"Yes," Margo responded.

"Who is 'them'?" I asked.

"Oh, I think you know them well. How do you think they survive? Children like those little monster Blackhearts."

"I see," I said, though I really didn't.

"That young boy, the one from playtime a few nights ago. Jasper? Do you know how they caught him? He was arrested with an illegal muse of dragonka while meeting a Kina trafficker under the Karlow Bridge. He knew their fate would be in the tanneries or on the plates of a foreign fat cat. But, luckily, the Kina trafficker was actually a Boot agent in disguise."

I swallowed my objections.

"Tatiana, call the hour to attention."

"Minutes, get in a circle!" barked Tatiana. Again the class jumped from their seats, surrounded Miss Kavanova, and counted off. When it came to my turn, I counted too. "One Fifty," I shouted.

"Now we have a complete hour," said Miss Kavanova, as though that settled some unresolved question in her mind. "Class, what is a clock?"

"A heart without music!" the class answered in unison.

"One Fifty," she said, addressing me. "What is a clock?"

"A heart without music," I answered dutifully.

"Then let's go find some music! Let's make a heart today!" she said. "Class, take One Fifty on field duty today." A twitter of excitement rippled through the class. Field duty was obviously something special.

After we were dismissed from class, we parked ourselves in front of the mirror in our bunkroom. You would have thought the class was going to a ball, the way they fussed over their uniforms and hair, pulling it back in severe tight buns, then tucking it under their black caps. I imitated them, because now I wanted to seem as much a part of the troop as possible. When we were ready, we waited by the front door for Miss Kavanova to dispatch with us. She arrived and handed Tatiana an envelope.

"Read it when you are outside," she said. "And have fun!" With that she flung open the door, and we marched out.

WE FOLLOWED TATIANA out of the school gardens and to the winding streets beneath the Palace. The people of the city treated me differently now that I was a member of the Youth Guard: bodies made way, conversations hushed as we passed. It was as though our uniforms were a kind of armor that protected us against the gloom that now hovered over Pava; like we were angels spinning music above the storm clouds.

When we got to the market, we were given what we wanted for free. The vendors forced smiles at us as they handed us fruit and poppy buns, but I could sense the fear behind their gestures. Was I the only one who heard their grumbling behind our backs as we left? We took our breakfast to the Palace gates so we could watch the Boot Guard come and go. Tatiana picked out her favorite guards and swooned as though they were moving-picture stars. After some time, she read the envelope Miss Kavanova had given her. Her eyes flashed between the paper and me.

"What's in it?" asked Sonia.

"I don't want to tell you," she responded demurely.

"Come on! What are we supposed to do?" asked Margo.

"Jozseftown," she responded direly.

Then she handed the paper to me. One word was written there: *Luma*.

I must have looked shocked, because Tatiana put her hand on my knee, consolingly. "It is a rescue mission," she said.

"But how did they know?" I asked.

"Of course they know," she said. "They know where each and every Jozseftown dragonka is. It is just a matter of extracting them, like veins of gold in a dangerous underground mine. You pull too hard, and the whole thing will come tumbling down on you. It was only a matter of finding the right tool."

"That's what I am, isn't it?"

"What?"

"The right tool," I said.

"You can do a lot of good here," said Tatiana, evading my question. "I know we never really liked each other. But I have to tell you, this is the right thing to do. The way they are treating the dragonka. This is the only way to save them. My own beast, Sabadka, was personally selected by Archibald for the Palace collection. I know he is getting the best treatment, the best food, the best of everything."

"I tried to save Luma," I said.

"You still can," said Tatiana. "Just take us to him."

"I will," I said, wondering if playing along was going to get me in more trouble than I'd expected.

WE PLOTTED OUR INCURSION into Jozseftown. It was agreed that I would take off my Youth Guard badge and precede the group as a kind of scout. But before we stopped at the Jozseftown gate, Tatiana pulled a map from her waist pouch. She unfolded it and smoothed it out on the cobblestone in front of us. "I hate this map. It makes no sense. It follows the sewers, but what are all these other things?" she said, exasperated. Indeed, it wasn't just the sewer system on the map: I could see the demarcations of the routes of the pneumatic mail system, complete with a coded legend in the margins. Tatiana traced her finger over our route, apparently unaware that she held one of the last remaining maps of its kind, if not the very last. I don't know why I violently fought the urge to tell her what it was. My mouth only locked up when I tried.

"OK, Petra K—I mean, One Fifty—will lead us from a distance above ground, then we will go underground until we find the Blackhearts' lair." She looked slyly up at me, then back at the map again when she registered that I had noted her mistake. It crossed my mind that Tatiana was playing along as well. It was the first time I had ever seen her blush.

"I think I should handle the map," I said. "I mean, it might be easier for me to find the path there. After all, I am from Jozseftown."

"Yeah," she said, handing me the map. "I can't read this thing at all. I will make you the underground navigator. I am troop leader, so I have that power. Agent One Twenty, you have a city map, don't you?"

"Yes," Sonia responded.

Tatiana handed me the map. I folded it into my pocket and then began to play my part. I took my armband off and went into Jozseftown just as I had left: Petra K. Even in the short period I had been away, things had changed in the neighborhood. Posters of Archibald lined the street, like a thousand pairs of secret eyes spying on passersby. But there were so few passersby to speak of. It was like the place had been emptied of humankind. When I walked past open windows, they shut as if on their own. Curtains were pulled tight, and doors of shops slammed like the sound of falling dominoes behind me. The place looked drained of color and charm. I felt my heart strain, then immediately rebelled against that feeling. Feelings are sortable; you can take them and push them away if you like, or tweeze out the ones you want if you choose to. The problem is they don't really go away. That is what was happening to me as I passed through Jozseftown. Feelings that I didn't want, that didn't work like clockwork, were surfacing within me. I was angry, but I missed it here, too. Above all, I wanted to find and protect Luma, even if it meant sacrificing the Blackhearts.

I stopped at the sewer grate by the broken fish fountain. I looked behind me to make sure the others registered where I was. I pried the grate open with my fingers. I looked around me before descending down into the city's depths again. I could smell the familiar dankness, but it was somehow different. Like the rest of the neighborhood, the sewers appeared deserted. I should have been afraid there, but I felt no fear, only a justness and dedication toward my mission. I wondered where the other girls were, but at the same time felt no need for their support. I would handle the Blackhearts.

But, as it turned out, there was no handling to be done, because their lair was still deserted. A few empty potion bottles lay around, overturned on the damp floor. Otherwise there was no sign of them. I looked about hopelessly. I despaired I would never know where Luma had gone. Then I heard a noise behind me. I turned, expecting to find Abel or Rufus, but instead there was the small Kubikula girl, Sytia, the one Deklyn had greeted when we visited their camp. She looked both fearful and curious, and almost human in those capacities. I went to her, and she immediately flung herself at me, clinging to my chest and letting out a sorrowful wail.

"Sytia," I said. "What is wrong?"

Before she could answer, from down the sewer corridor a troop of Boot officers sprang forth. The first one tore the girl from me, while the rest stormed the room. They overturned the remaining mattresses and flung the empty vials against the wall.

"Where are the Blackhearts, Agent One Fifty?" a Boot officer I had never met before bellowed at me.

"I don't know," I responded. I looked around for the rest of my troop, but they were no longer behind me.

"Take the Kubikula," he said, turning from me to his colleague. "Let's see what she knows."

"She doesn't know anything; she can't even speak," I said. The officer made no indication that he had heard me. He merely continued surveying the empty room and shaking his head. He had expected more.

"I said, she can't talk," I repeated. "You shouldn't take her anywhere."

"Dirty Kubikula. Their days of subversion are numbered," he said. "And take her, too," he said of me. "A lot of good she has done for us," he added spitefully. It was then that I knew I had been used. The girls were never going to show up. It was part of a plan that they had kept from me. Like Tatiana said: I was a tool, and had been used as such.

They threw us into the back of a Boot cart again. Sytia crawled to me and shivered against my side. Though I found her a bit repulsive, especially in the sunshine, where her skin looked unnaturally green and scaly, I pulled her close to me to give her comfort. I had little to give but I gave it anyway. She cried silently on my shoulder, shielding her eyes from the light.

I suppose it was my own fault for finding myself where I was. If I had "played along" from the start, as Bianka suggested, I am sure I would have been treated as an equal by the Youth Guard. If I had been more generous in my judgment of the Blackhearts, they might have accepted me as one of their own, instead of treating me like a strange, foreign cousin. But I had no choice but to be Petra K—and if that meant being alone, then that is what I would accept.

When we arrived back at the Pava Youth Guard Facility, they had to tear Sytia from me, then carry her off over the shoulder of a large Boot officer. I was surprised that I was not taken from the cart as well, for more time in the Dream Chamber. Instead they closed the back door, pulled the hatch down, and we continued on our way. It was not long before I discovered that I was being taken toward the Palace. Then, the gated walls to the Palace itself were thrown open, and the cart was driven onto the grounds. There we stopped, and I was pulled out, lifted over a shoulder, and carried through a small back door of the great building. I was delivered to a room, then pushed inside. After the officer's footsteps receded down the hallway, I flew at the door, only to find it locked. When I realized I would not escape that way, I turned and looked around myself. There was no window, but there was a soft, well-dressed bed. In fact, it was the biggest bed I had ever been in, with pillows like a small mountain range across the head. Moreover, there were fresh-cut scarlet tulipan in a crystal vase, and a bottle of juniper-flavored soda water on the nightstand. I drank the soda greedily. After some time, I lay my head down and fell asleep.

LATER, WHEN I WOKE, I found a new clean dress on the clothing rack. Mine had become so ratty, there was nothing to do but accept the offering and put it on. But just who was offering it?

It was then that I heard a distant singing. Not that of human voices, but that of dragonka. I went to the door to better hear. Yes, there was a chorus of dragonka somewhere in the Palace! I twisted the knob, only this time I found it open. Out of the room I crept. Down the hall I snuck, toward the sound of the dragonka song. Soon I came to a door. The charm of the chorus was coming from behind it, so I pushed it open. I discovered that I was outside, and it was the dead of night. The autumn Pava air was cold and unmoving, as if petrified by the dragonka song. I started in the direction of the sound. As I wandered I realized I was in a sprawling garden. It was no doubt Archibald's private space: there were great lavendula plants straining toward the moon (unlike most flowers, they lived off moonlight), and winter *violettas* bursting in glowing, radiant purple. The moonlight gave everything a silver sheen like a fading photo still.

Down a side path I strode, drawn by the noises. Entering a huge courtyard revealed their source. I had come upon the greatest collection of dragonka I had ever seen. Some were restrained from the neck with leather collars, flying about in frustrated circles; others (smaller ones and kiš-dragonka) were kept in large pens and great heated glass terrariums. Some had burning, translucent bellies, which lit up the night, little orbs of wonder. I had never seen anything like it. The spectrum of colors was fantastic: every shade and type imaginable was held there. At my approach, their excitement grew. One—a small umber-red pup—raced up my shirtsleeve, desperate for attention. Others buzzed in the air, executing magnificent tricks, hoping I would notice them.

Tiny muses of kiš-dragonka burned luminescent in the night like fireflies, creating spectacular patterns in their confinement. I held the red dragonka that had jumped on me until it calmed.

Soon the melody of the dragonka song began to have an effect on me. Such was its charm that I didn't even feel myself go under—it just happened, as the song filled the garden—sudden and fluid, soft and numbing, like a scentless poison gas had been released in the air. First I concentrated on the feeling of content-edness that blazed in me. Then the song stoked the ember, fan-ning it until it grew and seeped into every part of my body. Just then I could see the words, even though the dragonka sang no lyrics: there was a kind of poetry everywhere—in every mundane piece of garden furniture: every rotten memory of betrayal and hurt had an integrity restored to it, every piece of grass and weed patch was ablaze with intricate design, and even the air—even its invisibility—was instilled with a unique prism of light. The notes of the song bounced around in my body, and I gave myself up to them totally. Feelings traveled though the air like spirits. There was happiness in front of me like an old doltish clown guffawing in my face; there was sadness, weirdly impish and charming, a black cape flying behind it like a flag. Then I was overtaken com-pletely by the charm of such a huge dragonka chorus.

But the feeling ended as soon as it began. There was some-body there, watching me in the garden.

"Do you like my collection?" asked a voice, sleek and icy as frost on my neck. The voice brought me out of my delirium, instantly and shockingly. I turned around. There was Archibald the Precious, silently observing me, his pale skin shining in the moonlight.

"It's incredible," I answered.

"The one you are holding is the pup of a Newt Ball cham-pion. A Javanese emperor offered me an island off the coast of his country in exchange for him. But there is no amount that would convince me to part with him."

"Aren't all dragonka forbidden?" I asked.

"These are safe," he said. "Because they were born after the fever outbreak. They are clean."

"The others are clean too," I countered.

"No," he said. "That is not true."

"This whole dragonka fever thing is a lie!" I said.

"I brought you here to play, not to argue with me," Archibald said, suddenly flushed with anger. "People think I am quite cruel, but as you can see, I have taken their welfare upon myself. I provide for them, I feed them in the way they are accustomed to. And all I ask is that they are available to me, for play. It is not a big request, is it?"

"And what about the ones that disappear. Where do they go?"

"Sacrifice is involved. A culling. That, after all, is how we arrived with these creatures. You see, we have a plan to *perfect* the dragonka. To elevate them beyond the point of pure beast. Can you imagine a dragonka that isn't finicky about its diet? That follows orders? That is no trouble at all to keep? Not to mention the military applications of such a beast."

"No. And I don't want to," I said.

"Well, it is not for you to concern yourself with," he said.

Archibald was dressed in his uniform. He seemed so adult right then; it made me fearful. His face had a metallic sheen, like he had been bled dry and pumped with mercury. There was something inhuman about Archibald. Also, he appeared unsurprised by my appearance in the garden. I realized then that I had been expected, if not led to this place.

"Why was my door left open?" I asked.

"Because I wanted you to see," said Archibald. "I wanted you to discover everything for yourself."

"But why? Why didn't I go back to the reeducation facility?" I asked.

Archibald went over to the tank with the kiš-dragonka in it and put his hand to the glass. They appeared curious, buzzing around his fingers as though they were flower pistils from which sweet pollen could be collected—then they dispersed in a flurry when they realized their mistake. Archibald appeared to regret the deception, one that he looked to have practiced before. He withdrew his hand and turned back to me.

"Because I wanted you to see what I am offering," he responded evenly. The dragonka that had slithered around my neck had fallen asleep. "He likes you," said Archibald, taking a small key from his wrist and releasing the beast from his collar. "Bring him inside where it is warmer. There is something I want to show you." Archibald began to walk toward the Palace. I followed, with no more thoughts of spirits or emotions, the dragonka snoring quietly around my neck.

We went into a large double door that looked out on the gardens. Inside, I found myself in a sumptuous room filled with soft pillows on the floor and automatons resting up against the walls. Crystal mood shards glowed on a table, which also held an army of toy soldiers, mid-battle, waiting to be directed. Other toys were hidden in the far reaches of the dark room, out of my view.

"Welcome to my room," said Archibald expansively.

"Wow!" I exclaimed.

"Shhhh," he hissed. "They will hear."

"Who?" I asked, but Archibald just shook his head, not wanting to tell.

"We can play, but we have to do it quietly," he said, taking the small dragonka from my neck and holding it up to view it in the moonlight that shot through the window.

"OK," I said, deciding it was better to humor him until I found out why I was here. Perhaps it was the dragonka charm, but the effect of the Dream Chamber had worn off, and I felt like myself again. Archibald had better watch out. "What should we play?"

He shrugged his shoulders, as if to invite me to present an idea.

"Don't you remember me?" he finally said. "That night in Jozseftown. You gave me a quince from your bag, even though you needed it for yourself."

"That was you? What were you doing in Jozseftown at night? Alone?"

"I do that sometimes," he said. "It is a secret I keep from *them*. I sneak out at night, looking for somebody to play with. But nobody ever asks. It can be so lonely here."

"What did you want to show me?" I asked.

"Come, I will take you," he said. And with that, Archibald the Precious took me by the hand, and together we strolled through the darkened corridors of the sleeping Palace. He was silent as we walked, which was good, because I was mesmerized by the wonders of his home. I had never seen such a well-appointed corridor: one could have made a comfortable home in it alone, with lounge chairs and velvet-covered walls. Paintings of past royalty lined the way, interrupted by Kina cisterns and vases. Eventually we came to a door, which opened onto a spiral staircase. We had to go one after the other to descend, Archibald having grabbed a lit candle from the hallway. When we got to the landing, he opened another door that led to a dark, dank smelling place. We were in the basement of the Palace now.

"What's down here?" I asked.

"My study."

We entered a room that appeared to be some sort of laboratory. On the walls were illustrations of enormous hearts in various state of dissection, and in beakers tiny organs bobbed about in bubbling water.

"What are they?" I asked.

"Hearts," he said. "We tried growing them, but it didn't work like we wanted. You need a body for the heart to serve, or else it won't grow. Hearts die if they don't give life to something else. It is kind of contrary, don't you think?"

"Yes," I agreed.

"But my real playroom is through here."

"Can I see?" I asked.

"No. That place is private and off limits. Besides, I think you have had enough excitement for one night. Let's go back upstairs."

"But I thought you wanted to play," I said, still curious about what else Archibald was hiding.

"I did. But it is late. I'm sleepy now," he said. "We can continue the tour tomorrow." We turned back, went through the laboratory and up the stairs.

"I am not sure I will be able to sleep," I said.

"Try this," Archbald said, and drew from his pocket a small metallic contraption that looked like the motor to a music box. He wound the tiny crank. When released a slight humming came, then the faint sound of dragonka singing in chorus. I had never seen or heard anything like it before.

"It will help you sleep," he said, putting the song box in my hand. That should have ended my first day at the Palace, but it didn't.

I CRANKED THE DRAGONKA SONG BOX, listened to its tune, and fell asleep easily. But in the middle of the night I was startled awake again. Though I couldn't see anybody, I knew I was not alone in the room. "Who's there?" I called, but got no response. I lit the bedside paraffin lantern with quivering hands, but it revealed no living being. Before too long, I cautiously closed my eyes. It was then that I sensed the presence again. I sat up, and felt a chill overtake me, though no breeze blew. But a gust *had* passed through me, like there was a lit candle in my heart that something was trying to blow out. The feeling was at once warm and clammy cold, provoking within me a powerful feeling of sorrow. I felt tears come to my eyes, and sadness like none I had ever felt before. "Petra K," a familiar voice said. I held my head back so as not to cry, then before I knew it the feeling was gone. I cranked the song box and was asleep again in moments.

Chapter 15

I woke up early the next morning with the sun shining through the gossamer curtains. It took me a moment to realize where I was. It is not every day you wake up in a palace.

No sooner did I rise than an aged woman in a maid uniform came gliding into the room with a cart loaded with breakfast food: poppy-seed rolls, honey challah, roast pumpkin wedges, and cured hams, with more juniper-flavored soda water. I ate heartily; it had been so long since I'd had a proper meal. The maid watched over me as I gorged myself, and when I had finished, she helped me dress, then escorted me from the room, through the Palace and out into the garden, where Archibald was already waiting. His face brightened at my arrival. The young dictator was happy to see me.

"I am so excited," he said. "I have such a great day planned for us." He clasped my hands in his. I immediately felt their coldness. It was like holding hands with a corpse.

"Did you eat well?" he asked.

"Very," I said.

"You can enjoy such meals anytime you want."

"Thank you."

"It is my pleasure," he said shyly. I wondered if he had ever had a real friend.

"Is it just you and the dragonka here, then?" I asked.

"And the Ministry of Unlikely Occurrences," he said. "It was really their idea to perfect the dragonka."

"Can't you tell me what that really means?"

"I shouldn't say," he said, with a mischievous grin. "I was planning on giving you a tour of the Imperial Gallery, but I can show you all about our experiments instead."

"OK," I responded.

He took me by the hands and led me into the Palace. He opened a door and we descended into a different part of the cellars than the one we had been in the night before. We entered a long corridor, which was lined with doors. There was a strong smell present, something like sulfur and molten copper.

Suddenly, Archibald's eyes rolled back in his head. He swooned, then tripped and fell down the last step. I jumped to assist him. He pushed me off, and picked himself up—he was not hurt, but he looked humiliated. He hid his face from me.

"It's OK," I said. "You can cry in front of me."

"I can't," he said.

"Why not? I cry all the time," I said.

"I want to. . . . I feel like I should, but something is missing, I cannot cry."

"Everybody can cry!" I said.

"I don't feel sad, though. Just blankness. I can't cry. My heart does not allow it."

"What has your heart got to do with it?"

"It . . . how can I say this? It is not my real heart. I mean, it is my heart. I own it, but it is not real. I know it sounds incredible."

"It does," I said.

"But it quits on me. It winds down and just stops ticking."

"You mean beating," I said.

"No, ticking," he said. "Listen." I put my ear against Archibald's chest. Indeed, I heard a ticking sound as though Archibald had an alarm clock rather than a heart.

"I don't feel like a tour any more," he said.

"That's alright," I said.

"Shall we play a game instead?" he said.

"Sure," I responded.

"This is my favorite; I used to play it all the time before I found my friends. It's called Haints and Saints. You are the Haint, you have to hide. I am the Saint, I will find you."

"But the Palace is huge!"

"That's why it's fun. We have all day."

HAINTS AND SAINTS? Only partly right. It was time to find the Haints—real Haints—and I had all day to do it. In particular, I wanted to find the one that had passed through me the night before, who had fanned such sadness in me. And so it began. I ran through the rooms of the Palace, throwing open any door I pleased, coming across luxuries beyond belief. The kitchen larders were filled with pheasant, wild boar, exotic truffles, and edible flowers. Ancient tapestries and paintings decorated the bedrooms, studies with silver-plated pens and mood shards everywhere. It was in a remote parlor that my eye caught a dark mood shard in the corner of the room. The shard was a dark amber color that quickly changed to black as I gazed at it. Only it wasn't a mood shard at all, but a black piece of silk that lifted from its place and hung in the air, fluttering as though in a breeze. Then the scarf elongated, until it was the size of a cape. It fluttered toward me, then over my head and out the door, as though beckoning me to chase it. I ran out of the room just in time to see it vanish down a circular stone stairwell. I chased it down the stairs into a dank cellar corridor.

Again I was apprehended by the smell of sulfur, molten metal, and incense. It was acrid and hurt my nose, but still the charm was too strong to resist. I spotted the cape, just before it disappeared through a door. I went to the door, to find it closed. Then from within the room, I heard an ungodly howl. And then I felt the charm, mixed in with the howling. Dragonka were behind that door, braying in misery. The black cape had led me here, for some reason. I turned the door handle, and entered a pitch-black room. The crying stopped as suddenly as it had begun, but I still felt the charm.

I heard footfalls approaching. Archibald's meek voice called my name, sounding like a ghost come to haunt me. His footsteps stopped outside the door. I heard the doorknob turn slowly: Archibald was coming in. I backed up and flattened myself against the wall. Archibald entered. He called my name, then, when he got no response, lit a paraffin lantern, sending an orange glow along what looked like a storeroom. A shot of terror raced down my spine when I registered what the light revealed. The walls were lined with dragonka. But they were not alive. They were in jars, preserved in liquid like specimens in some horrific museum. Archibald walked up and down the rows of shelves, appraising the jars as though admiring a much-loved collection.

In a surge of revulsion I lifted my arm to cover my mouth, trying to restrain a scream. But in doing so, I knocked a jar from its place with my elbow. The jar fell crashing to the floor. The smell of camphor and death filled the room. I saw the small dragonka lying amidst the shattered glass and preservatives. Its heart had been cut out. It was then that I actually did scream.

"Petra K," he said, turning in delight. "I found you!"

"What is this?" I cried. There were innumerable dragonka, all with their hearts cut from them.

"This is my playroom," he said. "I wanted to show you, but you found it on your own. These are all my favorites. I try to visit every day." Now I knew what was happening to the dragonka that disappeared from the streets. They were not taken abroad as we were told, but instead met their fate here in the laboratories under the palace.

"What do you want to know?" he asked earnestly. "I will tell you everything. I see you are upset, but it is all for the good of Pava. Just let me explain. Will you come upstairs, have a poppy bun, and listen?"

He did not wait for an answer; instead he took me by the hand and led me upstairs to the Palace ballroom, where he sat me in a huge chair. He picked up a glass of juniper soda and handed it to me. Recovering from my shock, I lashed out, knocking the glass from his hand.

"Tell me why I am here!" I demanded.

"Because I get lonely. Do you know something? When I was much smaller, I used to play Haints and Saints. But I had no one to play with. It may sound sad, but I could do it for hours, hiding and waiting. That was how I came to know the Palace so well. In time, I discovered places in the basement. Those were the best hiding spots. I wasn't afraid, because I felt like I wasn't alone. I began to dream of creatures, no, *people* living down there. The spirits communicated with me through my dreams. They beckoned me to help them, and I did. You see, there was a wall downstairs that was obviously concealing something. The spirits called me through it. All I did was chip away at it, and there they were. By doing so, I released them from a curse that kept them there. They promised to be eternally grateful. We have been caring for each other ever since."

"How do they care for you?" I said dubiously.

"They help me with my sickness," he said.

If there was one thing I knew for certain at that moment, it was that the Palace was haunted, and Archibald was being made deranged by that haunting.

"I want you to stay here," he said. "The Haints are nice, but not fun to play with. I think if I ask them they will let you. What do you think?"

I was about to open my mouth when I saw a thoughtful look pass over his face.

"Oh," he said placidly, as though his babysitter had caught him reading under the covers late at night. "Here they come."

"Here come who?" I asked, for I couldn't hear anything, and felt but a quiver in the air.

Then, into the room trod a stout, squat man in a centuries-old army uniform with a peacock-feathered hat. Behind him slinked a tall, thin man who appeared made of nothing but a shadow. Then came a low rumbling, which turned into an explosive clattering, and through the wall burst two warhorses carrying a chariot and a rider in a leather vest. Another two spirits sprouted up through the floor. Still others hovered over us on the ceiling, shimmering and quaking like storm clouds at night. Before long the room was filled with spirits from the past ages of Pava. They surrounded Archibald as though protecting him from me. One cradled Archibald in his arms, and before long the small dictator was fast asleep. Now it was just me and them.

"What is your business here, child?" the stout one demanded.

"We were playing," I said. My answer caused a ripple of low, heated chatter amongst them. Finally the stout one came forward again. "What were you playing?" he ventured. "*Exactly* what?" the tall shadowy one rejoined.

"Nothing," I stammered.

"Nobody plays nothing," the shadowy one said. "Everybody plays *something*."

I gulped. I had no answer.

"Where do you live?" one asked.

"I . . . I don't know," I responded.

"Have you any gold?" another asked, as though he was a beggar looking for food. Indeed, they all had a sickly look to them. Their ghostly limbs were deteriorating, and appeared moth-eaten.

"No," I said. "No gold here."

"Then what good are you?" he sputtered, and disappeared into the floor.

"Is she spirit or human?" the spindly one said to the stout soldierly one, who appeared to be the leader of the group.

"Human, of course," said one in the back.

"But there is something so familiar in her ghostly attractions," said the stout one. A spirit from the ceiling swooped down next to me and inhaled, smelling me. The Haint howled with disgust and retreated.

"She is human indeed," came a voice from behind. I turned to see Wormwood in a white lab coat.

"Then what is she doing here?" demanded the general.

"I knew it was a bad idea, but it was Archibald's wish," he replied.

"He is not allowed to wish!" said the stout general.

"He *is* the monarch," said Wormwood, in a voice of conciliation.

"Have her removed!" said the stout one.

"Archibald will not be happy," said Wormwood.

"Get him more dragonka. More mood shards. Anything but this girl."

"Very well," said Wormwood. He approached me and held out his hand. In it was a small peppermint. "Here," he said, offering it forth. But I was not so easily fooled. I turned to flee, only to find myself in the grasp of a Haint who had snuck up behind me. I struggled, but he held me tight as Wormwood pressed a handkerchief to my face. From it I smelled the sweet pungent smell of camphor. I kicked with all my might, but it was no use. I passed out in his arms.

Chapter 16

I awoke in a cage in the back of the same cart that had delivered me. I was delirious at first, but when I came to my senses, I could see that we were traveling at a quick pace on a road out of Pava. I poked my head up to see the thick neck of a Boot officer cracking a whip over the heads of a pair of mighty horses.

"Where are you taking me?" I called to him, but he didn't even turn to acknowledge my voice. I repeated my question to no avail.

"We are going to the mines," came a voice from behind me. I turned my head. The cart was loaded with cages just like the one I was in, all filled with children. I scanned them until I saw a face I recognized. "There we will be worked to death."

"Jasper!" I called. It was him, indeed, though he had lost weight, and his threadbare shirt allowed his Blackheart tattoo to show on his chest.

"How are you?" I asked.

"That is a strange question coming from you," he responded with bitterness in his voice. "You are one of the Boot Youth Guard. We know about you."

"I am not! It was you who betrayed the dragonka," I said.

"If that is what you think, I cannot stop you. But the traitor is *you*."

"If I was a traitor, what would I be doing here?" I countered.

"The only reason you are here is because the Boot kill their own if it suits them."

"You don't understand," I said. But I remembered the ceremony where he was treated with such violence. I had lost all trust of the Blackhearts, if I had ever really had it.

"I may go to my death with dignity. But you . . . you will die a coward," said Jasper.

I slumped in misery. Then a horrible thought jolted me. "Jasper," I finally said. "Jasper!"

"What?"

"Did the Blackhearts sell Luma?"

"Sell Luma?"

"For his skin," I said.

"Ha!" he guffawed. "Is that what you think?"

"I don't know what to think," I said.

"Well you will have plenty of time to ponder it in the mines. There they work you until you can no longer stand upright," he said.

"Stop with that talk. You are scaring the others," I said when I noticed a small Half Not child listening in.

We stopped speaking. A dread wound its way between all of us, like a snake amongst sleepers. It was freezing cold, and I held myself tight to keep from shivering too much. It wasn't until the cart came to a lurching halt that I looked up again.

"Get out of the road!" the driver shouted. I pressed my head against the top of the cage to see what was holding us up. There in the middle of the road was a small potbellied pig. "Rufus!" I began to yell, but my voice was cut short by Jasper, who grabbed me through the bars. He shook his head gravely. I turned back to watch. The driver stood up to threaten the pig.

Rufus stood his ground, then began to grow! He was puffing up, as though he was a balloon and somebody was filling him with air. Suddenly, when he was the size of a cow, he burst, and gold coins went flying everywhere.

"What?" the driver exclaimed in disbelief. Then he began to chuckle when the coins showered around him. He sprung from the cab and began to gather the gold into his pockets, laughing and amazed. Stealthily, from behind a tree, a figure emerged. Deklyn leapt into the cab and yanked the reigns hard, taking control of the confused horses. Isobel too emerged from hiding and jumped into the back of the cart. In a flash, Deklyn had the cart moving. We circled the confused Boot officer. He made a few stumbling grasps for the reigns, but Deklyn was too fast. In an instant, we were back on the road to Pava, galloping full speed. We stopped briefly, and Rufus jumped into Deklyn's arms. No doubt the gold had turned to clay by now, and the Boot officer was cursing his birth star.

As we fled, Isobel climbed nimbly amongst the cages, releasing us one by one. All the other children clamored to get to the front of the cart and pat Deklyn on the shoulder. We were free. With the wind rushing about us, it felt like we were going to rush straight into the city and recapture it for the people. But Deklyn stopped short of the city border.

"Everybody out!" he yelled. "We have to continue underground." Children who had looked so distraught and lifeless before now jumped from the cab with savage howls. Once settled, Deklyn took them one by one, and, with a piece of black charcoal, drew a black heart on each of their chests.

"Honorary member," he said to each, then directed them toward a drainage pit by the river. I ran to Deklyn to congratulate him.

"That was amazing," I said.

"Not bad for somebody who just sells fake potions. Isn't that what you said?"

"That was before."

"Before what? Before you betrayed us?"

"I did not," I said. But I knew if Jasper didn't believe me, Deklyn wouldn't either.

"It does not matter now," he said. "We can't trust you, so you can't come this way. Go overland. And when you see your Youth Guard friends again, tell them the JRM was well at work." He looked at me with spite. And without another word, the small gang disappeared into the darkened underground passage. But after the crowd disappeared into the darkness, Isobel re-emerged. She approached me.

"I know you are innocent," she said. "I see things the others don't. They only understand force and blood. But keep out of Jozseftown. Things are dangerous there if you are not part of the JRM. I will talk to Deklyn and send word to you."

"Agreed," I said. "And, thanks." Isobel gave my hand a squeeze, looked me in the eye, not without kindness, and then disappeared down the tunnel.

OF COURSE I WAS GOING to go straight back to Jozseftown, for the simple fact that I had nowhere else to go. I made my way quietly, trying to keep to back streets where I would not be spotted. Boot guards stood at every corner. It was as though they had multiplied in my absence. I slipped quietly among them. Before long I was at the Jozseftown gate. What I really wanted to do was to go home. I could feel the pull of my mother, but I suspected she would send me back to where I had just escaped from. Instead, I followed a feeling that rose from my gut, a feeling that told me I needed to go to Jozseftown Cemetery. If Zsofia was still there, I knew we could help each other. I needed a friend. The only question was: was she still alive?

After scaling the wall, I found the mausoleum into which I had last seen her disappear. I pulled the door open and entered quietly. The dry, dark space was empty; there was no sign that

Zsofia was still residing there. I had no better idea, so I decided to make this my shelter for the time being. If the Blackhearts could do it underground, I could survive here, if I wanted to. The only question was: did I want to? If anybody has ever encountered a livable cemetery, I would like to know about it.

I made a nestlike bed of my jacket, and pushed shut the stone door on the wind. It was a cold but bearable abode. I had escaped the mines, but I still didn't know why the Palace was rounding up the dragonka and what Luma had to do with the whole thing. Whatever the answer was, I knew Luma had something special about him that never failed to arouse curiosity. At least I was safe, and hidden where I was. I let out a sigh of relief.

It was then that I felt a hand grasp my ankle.

In an instant I was yanked downward and dragged through a hidden trapdoor. I landed with a thud on a pillow. It took me a few moments to rub the dirt from my eyes, but when I did, there before me sat Zsofia, in a white lab coat. And behind me, with her webbed-fingers on my shoulder, the person who had apprehended me: Ludmilla. Carmine- and mint-colored bats fluttered around my head.

"Welcome to my new laboratory," she said.

Chapter 17

In the tradition of refugees, mutants, and criminals on the run, Ludmilla had taken shelter in Jozseftown after the Boot closed her shops. There, she had set up a miniature laboratory. The grim space had been transformed into a white gleaming room; alabaster busts of Ludmilla's ancestors stood in the corners, portraits of noble women from abroad, all former clients, graced the walls. In the center of the room stood barrels of clay from the Pava River, which she used in her mudpacks.

The Newt doorman who had once worked at her department store bowed to me, tipping his hat, only now he wore a casual smoking jacket.

"Have a look around," she said. "Try a sample, though I fear a youth-enhancing pack would put you in diapers."

"Who do you sell these to?" I asked, astonished at what I saw.

"Oh, I still have my clients," she said. "It is only the method of distribution that has changed, thanks to this one," she said, indicating Zsofia. Ludmilla busied herself packing a round cartridge with an order of mudpacks. "You see?" she asked, indicating a tube that ran along the floor, and a mechanism with levers, like a large typewriter. It was the pneumatic mail system!

"Sorry," Zsofia said to me. "I don't have time to catch up. There is a blocked tube somewhere under the river, and I have to go unblock it."

"It must be another rat. They love the pneumatic tubes. It is like a carnival ride for them," said Ludmilla.

"Can I come?" I asked.

"Do you want to?" said Zsofia, grabbing my hand and grinning. I was glad to have her back as a friend.

"Of course," I said.

"Only, bring Petra K back. I have to talk to her," Ludmilla said.

"How could I possibly lose her?" Zsofia asked. They looked at each other and cracked up in laughter.

"Sorry," said Ludmilla. "It is just that the system of tunnels is so very complicated, and the glow clouds are growing dimmer by the day."

"Might a map help?" I asked.

"Of course," Ludmilla said. "But they just don't exist anymore."

"Well, actually," I said, pulling the map from my pocket and unfolding it in front of them. Ludmilla looked over the map, then gasped.

"This opens up whole new markets," she said.

"And it has the codes," I said, turning it over.

"Codes!" she shrieked, as though I had just dumped a pile of pink diamonds in front of her. "Petra K, what do you want for this? I'll give you anything."

I considered for a minute. "Get my mother some tea. Oolong. It is her favorite. And maybe something nice from your lab. And, I want a copy of the map for myself."

"Consider it done," Ludmilla said.

"Come on, Petra K," said Zsofia. "Let's go find that rat."

Zsofia had a small flock of glow clouds at her disposal. They bunched together like a fistful of cotton balls shot through with electricity. She raised a flute to her mouth and the glow clouds came to attention around us.

"Were you here all this time, in the cemetery?" I asked.

"Yes," she said. "Ludmilla took me under her wing when she realized it wasn't us who were responsible for the tainted perfume getting out."

"Then who was it?"

"Tatiana. She was a spy for the Boot long before she was inducted into the Youth Guard."

"But she got sick," I said.

"True, but she knew all along that would happen. She planted the perfume in your gift bag herself. They needed somebody who had no Palace connections. And, that was you. She knew she would get sick, she knew there was an antidote waiting from the Ministry of Unlikely Occurrences. She knew she would be made captain of the Youth Guard when the time came."

"Wow," I said. "But what about the perfume I smelled in the mausoleum?"

"Totally harmless. Want to try?" Zsofia took from her pocket a bottle of the black perfume and pointed it at me.

"No!" I screamed, jumping back.

"If you can't trust me, how can I trust you?" she said. "We know you were in the Youth Guard."

I took the vial from her hand and examined it. I drew a deep breath, and sprayed it against my neck. The same molten wax and musky smell overtook me that I remembered from Ludmilla's laboratories. I handed it back to Zsofia. I waited for a few tense moments; and felt nothing but silly for wearing perfume in the sewers of Pava.

"Ludmilla would never poison children. It is bad for business, as you can see."

"But why did they sabotage her?"

"You know she comes from a long line of sorceresses. Well, her ancestor, the original Ludmilla, was the one that put the curse on the Haints, keeping them bound in the Palace laboratories like slaves. It is revenge that was a long time coming. Now let's keep moving."

The glow clouds illuminated the path ahead of us. Beneath Pava was a strange, mysterious place. Aside from the Kubikula, it was wholly unexplored. "The things I have come across down here," she mused. "An albino python that glowed in the dark, a troupe of exiled Sibernian gnomes, and a crazy amount of bones. Ludmilla likes the bones; she grinds them up for face scrubs. If her customers only knew. . . ."

"How did you come to work for her?"

"Well, she found me the same way she found you. I was wandering sick with the dragonka fever through Jozseftown. The only refuge I found was in that mausoleum. She brought me into her lab, and cured me of the sickness, then put me to work. I'm learning how to concoct all kinds of great stuff. We are actually making our own antidote to the dragonka fever from the same perfume. That was my idea."

During the course of our walk, Zsofia talked so much about her job that I lost track of where we were, though the dank smell led me to believe we were somewhere under the Pava River.

"Here we are," she said, stopping at a portion of the glass tube that ran above us. "Look, you can see that something is trapped there, blocking the path."

"Now what?"

"Simple, I unclog it," she said. She pulled a wrench from her bag, found the place where the pipes were joined, and undid the screws on the joiner. She carefully lifted the glass from its place, laid the tube on the sewer floor, put on a glove, and reached toward the problem. "Stupid rats," she said. "Always joyriding. I can't tell you how many times I have had to rescue one like this. Rats are actually smarter than people give them credit for . . . for instance they—" Before she could finish, Zsofia screamed. She pulled her arm from the pipe, and hanging off the end of her glove was a small dragonka, except this one had two heads, one of which appeared to be fashioned from gold and was biting into the finger of my friend.

"Quick, open the bag!" she yelled at me. I did so, and Zsofia shook her hand until the creature fell from her arm and into the open pouch. I quickly zipped it up, sealing the creature inside.

"God," she said, rubbing her hand. The glove had protected her skin from the fangs, but it still looked like it hurt. "What was that?"

"They come from the Palace," she said. "They are getting more vicious and ugly all the time. Let's get it back to Ludmilla, and quick." We made haste in reattaching the glass tube, and followed the glow cloud back to the mausoleum entrance.

IT WAS A TASK, extracting the wild beast from the bag and getting it into a terrarium. The dragonka was not at all grateful for its release; it snarled up at us, its tiny fangs flashing in the paraffin light. Ludmilla dropped a chloroform-soaked cotton ball in with it. Soon the beast got drowsy, then toppled over, asleep. Ludmilla took it by the tail and held it up for examination. "There is nothing remotely natural about this. Can you feel the chill it gives off? In place of a charm? The magic used to create it is the imperfect work of charlatans."

"Because it comes from the inside," I said. "The magic."

Ludmilla looked impressed. "Yes," she said. "Are you by chance part Half Not?"

"No," I said.

"Oh, well never mind."

"They are breeding them in the Palace," I informed her, eager to help. "The Haints are performing experiments on the dragonka up there. Archibald says they are trying to *perfect* the dragonka."

"Perfect them into what?" said Ludmilla. "Killers? Machines of war? What else are those bitter spirits doing up there?"

"They are growing hearts."

"I know about that. They tried to get my help, blackmailing me with my stores as bait, but I refused. It would be reputation ruining. It can't be easy to create a heart, even with their black magic, but that has been the mission of the Ministry of Unlikely Occurrences since their inception."

"They are the Haints," I said. "The Ministry of Unlikely Occurrences."

"You're quick," she said. "Now, let's see exactly what they are up to. Zsofia, bring me a scalpel." Zsofia complied, finding Ludmilla a sharp, unused blade. Ludmilla turned the sleeping dragonka over. On its chest was a scar.

"If you are squeamish, I suggest you turn away," she said to me. "Don't worry about the dragonka, it is not much more than machinery and body tissue. Its spirit departed long ago." She made a quick incision and pulled back the gold scales. I gazed at the specimen, now sliced open. Inside the dragonka was not a heart but a clocklike contraption. "That is why they have no charm. They have no heart."

"But they are growing hearts in the Palace."

"Maybe, but not for the dragonka," said Ludmilla.

"For Archibald!" I said, making the connection with Archibald's story. "They need a heart for Archibald."

"That might be," agreed Ludmilla. "If they can put a mechanical heart in a dragonka, they can put a dragonka heart in a child. But they would have to incubate it in a living body."

"It's Luma!" I said. "Luma is growing Archibald's heart!"

I understood everything now. That was why Luma had such strange energy, and why they were eviscerating dragonka. They were looking for the right heart. The one I had all along. Or, the one Luma had, I should say. Now, with that heart, Archibald would live forever, the Haints would rule over Pava for perpetuity.

And the people would do their bidding—controlled through an army of vicious charmless dragonka.

"That's what Luma is," she said. "An experiment gone *right*, after so many tries."

LUDMILLA INVITED ME TO STAY, offering me shelter and a job with her. As much as I wanted it, I had far greater obligations. I needed to find my dragonka. The Newt doorman gave me the copy of the map he had copied, then showed me the route out—through a mausoleum floor and from an empty grave. I fled the graveyard at top speed, dodging the gravestones, jumping over flowers that were laid over the resting places of the dead, and out onto the streets. I hastened through my old neighborhood, Jozseftown, which I had never seen so quiet. Nobody was on the streets now, not even the shops were open. Only empty stalls populated the markets, letting the wind whistle around the cold bare metal. On the walls, instead of posters of Archibald, black broken hearts were scribbled in chalk or paint. I saw the Blackhearts' symbol everywhere.

On Goat Square I paused by the street that led to my house. My mother was there, languishing inside, cold and alone. Even after she abandoned me, I could not help but feel pity for her, wondering if she had enough food and hoping she still had tea to get her through the day. But I could only spare a brief thought for her. I needed to find Deklyn and, most of all, Luma.

As it happened, I would not have to find them: they would find me. One moment I was walking down the cobblestone street, the next I was being hoisted into the air, caught in the net of a trap. In a flash I was surrounded by children with JRM arm patches.

"Aww," one of them said. "I thought we had a Boot Youth Guard in our hands."

"Wait!" called another. "I know her." I spotted Abel. "Let her down!" The net was lowered. I fought my way to a standing position to face him. I immediately noticed a change in the boy. He now assumed an air of authority, like he had grown a few sizes in my absence. The others in his group, none of whom I recognized, fell in behind him, waiting for his command. I struggled with the net, and finally exhausted myself, still entrapped. Abel waved.

"Where is Luma?" I asked.

"He is safe," said Abel. "He is doing real well as Luma the Illuminator. We have buckets of money. Of course it all goes to the JRM, but I got a stuffed frog of my own!"

"I know that's not entirely true," I said.

Abel looked away. "Fine, he hasn't won a tournament since you disappeared."

"We had a deal," I said, "the Blackhearts and me."

"I know," Abel said.

"Besides," I said, "there is something I need to deliver to Deklyn. It will help the resistance."

Abel considered this. "OK, let her out. You know that Deklyn is the most wanted person in Pava now. His raids on Boot warehouses are the stuff of legend. The Boot has offered a ten-thousand kuna reward for him."

"Then he shouldn't be afraid of me, should he?" I said.

"I don't know why I like you, Petra K, but I do," he said, smiling.

I was blindfolded, and led by him and his troop through the streets of Jozseftown. The others pushed me when I didn't walk fast enough. They probably thought I was still in the Youth Guard.

I was led through a door and into a room. I was left alone—still blindfolded, but it appeared as though I had been deserted. There was a familiar smell in the air that I was trying to place, when I heard a voice.

"It's OK, you can take it off now." It was Deklyn. I removed my blindfold. He was there, behind a huge oak desk, with my map of the pneumatic mail system spread out in front of him. "Look," he said, pointing to a coordinate. "We can make contact with the province resistance beyond the Palace by sending a message *here*. And the Newt Resistance, *here*. We can coordinate everything with this map. It is even more essential than I thought. The pneumatic system goes everywhere!"

"That's mine!" I said, realizing they had surreptitiously emptied my pockets.

"Actually, the inventor of the underground mail delivery system—who now rests in the Zsida cemetery—was a friend of the Blackhearts. This map was *his* first, property of Jozseftown second. So it will be used by the people of Jozseftown. It *belongs* to us. Not to you."

"I am from Jozseftown," I said. For the first time, I felt proud of that fact. "I am a Jozseftown daughter too."

"Then why did you betray us?"

"I didn't. I only wanted Luma back."

Deklyn took a deep contemplative breath.

"You can go, Petra K. I believe you."

"I don't want to go," I said.

"Do as you like," said Deklyn. "Sytia told me about how you helped her. Just don't get too near Jasper. He doesn't trust you. But I guess he never did."

"Take me to Luma," I said.

"Luma," he said absentmindedly.

"Yes," I said, taking the map from his hands. "I want to see my dragonka."

"Tonight, perhaps," he said. "At the League of the Maiden and Minor Pup."

"He is still competing?" I was outraged.

"We are barely able to feed ourselves, thanks to that beast's losses. Forget about buying new weapons or fighting automatons. We should have sold him to a leather tanner long ago."

"You wouldn't," I said.

"No. I was kidding," Deklyn said.

"Take me to the tournament tonight."

"All the JRM will be there," he said. "If you told anybody, it would be the end of us."

"I can help Luma win, this one last time," I said. "You'll get the money you need."

Deklyn looked down, considering. Finally he met my eyes. "Find me by the fountain with the broken fish. We will go together underground."

"OK," I said.

"Here," he said, handing me a winter pear. "Have something to eat." And with that he got up to leave the room.

"Wait!" I said. "Where am I?"

Deklyn guffawed. "Don't you recognize your own house?"

I WALKED THROUGH THE DOOR and breathed in the stale but familiar smell. The hovel had fallen into further disrepair. I could only wonder where my mother was, and what Deklyn was doing there.

But as I descended the stairs I knew what would happen: I would knock on my mother's door. She would instinctively know who it was and call me in. She would be in bed: uncared for, filthy, but still alive. The sight of me would revive her, however. Her arms would open as I ran to her. And then we would be reunited. She would beg forgiveness, and I would forgive. It would be nothing at all. I longed to do just that, in fact: relieve her guilt.

But I could not open the door. It was as though some dark spirit held my arms at my side, preventing me from reaching for the knob. It is the worst thing I have done, not going in. That was my real betrayal. Half my heart was on the other side of that door, but right then I couldn't do anything to mend it.

THAT AFTERNOON I BATHED for the first time in days. I put on fresh clothes from my closet. I suspected that even though I had escaped the Boot, they still might know where I was, and could show up at any moment to spirit me away again. But I needed to feel at least a bit normal, if I was going to be ready for the trial ahead.

The Jozseftown clock chimed the time. I was late. I grabbed my coat and ran from the house.

Chapter 18

When I arrived at the broken fish fountain, I found the place deserted. I was too late. In frustration I kicked a fallen twig. But, from a dark causeway, two figures appeared. It was Abel, Rufus by his side. "What 'cha doing?" he asked. I could have kissed him, that sweet little grubby face.

"Waiting for Deklyn," I said.

"He couldn't come," Abel said, almost shyly.

"What's wrong, Abel?" I asked.

"Sorry," he said. "Sorry for catching you in a net and not letting you out."

"It's OK," I said.

"I can take you to the tournament, if you like," he said.

"Yes," I replied. "That would be great."

ABEL LED ME THROUGH a maze of streets. Along the way I discovered that the neighborhood was not as deserted as it seemed. Once we got near the graveyard I noticed shops that were open, selling marionettes, or repairing automatons as though nothing had ever changed. Shopkeepers greeted Abel; one threw him a candied apple, which he handed to me. I had not realized how hungry I was until that moment. I devoured the fruit greedily, tossing the whittled core to Rufus.

How fascinating the ghetto was to me even in its degraded state: this was the place where I belonged; amidst the Zsida students who were lost in holy books, mumbling prayers as they walked, black shawls trailing like great wings, which might lift them skyward at any moment; and the Half Nots who frequented the betting galleries. We walked amongst the traders who kept their stalls huddled together, as if for protection against winds that heralded destruction. And the things they sold were like none other: I saw strange astrological charts where the planet was resting atop a coiled, three-headed serpent; hats made of fur that made the wearer look like an upright bison; and bottles that contained blazing fires. When the proprietor caught me gazing at them he picked one up, tossing it from hand to hand to show it did not burn, then opened the bottle, poured some into a glass, tipped it back, then blew a ring of fire into the night. This was my home, and I was a part of it.

Abel led me further into the district. We soon came to an enormous old tenement, the entrance adorned with a frieze of a nude woman who had the head of a dove. The doors were open, so Abel escorted me in, Rufus running ahead in excitement. Inside I was surprised to hear the rumble of a crowd. It was amazing to me that anybody was having a festival of any sort at this time; it seemed the neighborhood itself was reflected in Abel's indomitable spirit.

BUT THIS TOURNAMENT was somehow different from the others. The first thing I noticed was that only children were there. They were divided into groups, which I soon recognized as separate gangs. Abel explained, "Over there are the Big Thumb Devils. Next to them are the Stink Clovers. Disgusting bunch. Lots of former government kids. You might like them, but they deal in dragonka trafficking. That's when they sell dragonka in another country."

"I know," I said.

"*Sorry*," he said sarcastically. "Then there are some kids who haven't joined anybody, because they don't want to or they couldn't get in. Some of them are just waiting to see who's got the best stock, and they'll try to join with them. Others are here just cause they got nowhere else to go. You know, like you."

I looked at him hard, but he was right.

"There are no Zsida, no Half Not elders; there are no adults at all," I said.

"They are all hiding in their homes. They gave up, for fear of arrest. It is only us who care now."

"And where is Luma?" I asked, looking around.

"Being prepared by Isobel, I imagine."

"Take me to him."

Abel looked doubtful for a moment before agreeing. He led me up a staircase and through the door into the former custodian's quarters. No sooner did I enter the room than Luma flew from Isobel's clutch, homing in on me, and almost toppling me over when he used my body to break his flight. I held him tightly to my chest. It was like our hearts were two magnetized halves that had come together. And how splendid he had turned out—when I thought of the sick little pup I had plucked from the wet sack. Now, he seemed to be thriving in the squalor and mystery of Jozseftown.

"First," I said, "take these silly sequins off him. He is a champion, not a minnow." Isobel did as I said without protest. "Now, leave us alone." Isobel quietly shooed Abel from the room.

I held Luma before me and looked into his eyes. My breathing quickened, and I felt the blood race as my heart quickened to meet the pace of my dragonka's. But it was more than our hearts beating at the same pace: a part of me now inhabited Luma, and a part of Luma inhabited me. I felt myself becoming one with him in the instant before the start of the race. When Luma would be flying up there, so would I.

The infinite depth of the dragonka's gaze was broken by Abel's voice.

"Come on," he said. I took Luma and descended the stairs to the courtyard. "We're going to start after we burn some toys."

"Burn toys?"

"It's a sacri*fire*."

"You mean a sacrifice?"

"I mean sacrifire. It's what I said."

As we walked down the stairs, Abel explained.

"Deklyn says there will be time for toys only after Pava is free of Archibald and the Boot. Terrible, but that's the way it is. It's how we begin the races these days. Just watch."

We joined the crowd. I didn't recognize anybody, so I waited next to Abel. Then from their group one child stepped forward and ran toward me.

"Petra K! I can't believe it's you." It took me a moment to recognize Margo. Her clothing was in tatters, and she looked like a kitchen girl who spent her days peeling potatoes and hauling coal.

"Petra K," she said. "I can't believe you escaped."

"What are you doing here?"

"I couldn't play along anymore. They are killing dragonka."

"I know."

"And they expected us to participate. It is sick."

"I saw it, too," I said, putting my hand on her arm to comfort her.

"Come stand with us, I am sure you will find some friends," offered Margo, indicating the Stink Clovers, the gang she had apparently joined. At this invitation, Abel perked up his head, interested about how I would respond. I realized I was being given a choice. I slowly shook my head and put my arm around Abel. "I'd better stay over here," I said.

"Suit yourself," said Margo. "The festival is about to begin, so I should get back." Without another word she rejoined the Stink Clovers.

FORTHWITH, A BONFIRE WAS BUILT, blazing up toward the stars. Of course no fire in Jozseftown was entirely free of the neighborhood's charms: it flared and whipped like it was alive. Invisible spirits danced around the flame, exciting it into a fury, feeding off its energy and heat, lonely and outcast from the world, bored and bleeding it for anything they could. The air was infused with a tension that made the gangs excitable, and every movement and word spoken was filled with significance.

It was Deklyn who stepped to the fire first. He carried a rocking horse in his hands. It struck me as odd that they should be burning valuables when there was nothing but poverty around them, but in a way it was fitting: these kids who all came from broken homes, discarding what they should have cared for, just as they had been discarded. Like the dragonka they kept, they were living within their most honest impulses, defying logic and good sense.

"In the name of the Blackhearts, grant us luck!" Deklyn shouted. With that, he tossed the rocking horse onto the fire. A cheer rose from the crowd: a wild, animal sound. The toy ignited instantly and was soon blackening into char. A girl, the leader of the Stink Clovers, brought forth a music box, opening it to show a tiny, twirling dancer.

"In the name of the Stink Clovers, an offering for luck in the races!" A flame appeared to whip out from its place and snatch the box from the girl's hands, drawing it back hungrily in to its belly. But the biggest cheer came when a Big Thumb Devil took from a pillow case a barking automated Kina dragonka (that the metal would only scorch did not matter) and threw it into the blaze, where its rice *benzin* cartridge exploded in a shower of sparks.

"Who are they sacrificing the toys to, anyway?" I asked Abel.

"The spirits of dead dragonka," he said, shrugging his shoulders. "I don't get it. I kind of liked that rocking horse."

"I'm sure you'll get one someday," I said.

"I don't want any stupid toys, anyway," Abel said in an abrupt burst of anger, kicking the dirt, then stomping over to the Blackhearts. I didn't understand what I had said wrong, except that maybe life was more difficult for Abel here than I had presumed. I didn't have time to dwell on it; the tournament was about to start.

THE FESTIVITIES BEGAN STUPENDOUSLY. A team of clownish dragonka trained to walk on stilts came out and entertained the crowd with their pratfalls. They were followed by a display of unique dragonka the gangs had collected: there was a snakelike dragonka that terrified everybody as it was released from its cage and squirmed along the floor in pursuit of a small goat, sacrificed for the occasion. Next a team of uniformly cloned pink dragonka pulled a sleigh around the ring with a tiny figure of Archibald, drawing howls of laughter from the audience. Behind them came an acrobat juggling three balls. When he held them up to the light it was revealed that there were kiš-dragonka trapped in the plasma-filled orbs, like little planets of fireflies.

As the races began I realized something: I had missed the excitement of the competition. My mind was not on Archibald, on the Youth Guard, or even on my mother. The sheer thrill of it all overtook me completely. It was because Luma was a part of me—I was sharing his anticipation. Let what would happen, happen, so long as Luma won. And then, suddenly, it was our turn. Luma looked out into the ring with a determination that brought a rush of joy and pride to my heart. I took him on a walk around the ring, so the audience could decide how they wanted to bet. There were shouts of encouragement and a few jeers from the camps of opposing dragonka, but Luma seemed to absorb all the attention, if not feed off of it.

I left Luma in the ring. A larger dragonka was brought out, and the ringmaster cracked the whip, signaling the beginning of the mock-joust. The opponent, Agascus, proved worthy from the opening moments of the contest, circling Luma with an unsettling coolness. Luma began to gnash his teeth at Agascus, which was not a good sign: being made aggressive too early, before the creatures had even taken flight. It was Luma who took to the air first, perhaps to get out of a gambit he was losing. Agascus soon followed, continuing his spiraling strategy, always keeping Luma in front of him. Luma had learned a lot from Isobel and he was able to rotate himself in mid-air with ease, ending each turn in a pose that the audience applauded. Luma, unlike the cunning Agascus, had form, and because of it he won over the audience. This, of course, was another strategy, and it began to work. Agascus was quick to anger, hurt that the audience was not siding with him. I realized what a powerful tool it was, and why Isobel had concentrated so much on Luma's form and poses. He looked magnificent up there, as though being manipulated by an expert puppet master.

But soon things took a turn for the worse. Agascus changed his strategy, staring Luma straight on in the eyes. Luma rose to the challenge, and the two squared off, their wings beating gently to keep them aloft. The crowd became quiet and the air tensed. I realized that I was holding my breath, and had to remind myself to inhale. No two dragonka could stare into each other's eyes for long without one losing control and attacking. It was a matter of moments.

It was Agascus who lost control first, making a charge at Luma. But Luma, also lost in the contest, instinctively moved out of the way, allowing Agascus to miss his protective collar, and therefore remain in the match. But at the last moment he regained his concentration and gave the other dragonka a tap on the rump with his tail as he passed. It was a dangerous move, one the judges might well have deemed an attack, costing him the match—but the judges were experienced and realized it was but a taunt, and one that worked because Agascus made another run, this time fixing his teeth firmly on Luma's neck. That ended it: Luma won again, and the crowd rewarded him with an explosion of applause. It was an excellent showing.

LUMA HAD WON HEAVILY AGAIN. This time I said nothing when Deklyn collected the winnings for the Blackhearts. Luma himself was quite content, if not a bit smug, soaking up the adoration of the other children who crowded around my able, young beast. I extracted him from their midst and took Luma over to feed him on a dish of rose water and pomegranate seeds.

"I am taking him home," I said to Deklyn, who had joined us there.

"No," stated Deklyn. "And don't argue. It is too important now to quibble over. He is safer with us."

"But I need him. Besides, I have *nobody*."

"You were true to your word, so you can stay with us, too," he said almost offhandedly. Feeling emotion well up in my eyes, I hid my face from his sight.

Chapter 19

The Blackhearts' new lair was in an abandoned build-ing near the center of Jozseftown. There was plenty of room, and their stock of dragonka made the most of it: racing down the hallways and shooting from the windows like cannonballs. Luma had grown in the short time I was gone; he was almost full grown, and, I imagined, so was his heart. I kept the part about Archibald's experiments with growing hearts a se-cret, because if Deklyn knew, well, I am not sure what he would have done. I couldn't take the chance that he would kill Luma outright. I was Luma's protector, and that meant protecting him from the Blackhearts as well.

THE FOLLOWING EVENING I was trying to fall asleep on the bed of blankets they had given me. I glanced over to where Deklyn was sleeping, without really meaning to look at him. He was so confi-dent and stubborn, it was aggravating; but somehow I kept look-ing his way, then catching myself and looking away awkwardly.

"What is it, already?" he said.

"It's just . . ." I was about to say that I understood him. I understood about losing parents—or feeling like you don't have them at all. That I felt a shadowy black heart—similar to his—hovering over my own breast. But before I could start, Isobel came rushing into the lair.

"Wake up!" she called, shaking Abel awake.

"What?" said Deklyn, rubbing his eyes.

"It's Jasper. He has gone crazy. He is out on Goat Square shouting all kinds of things about the Boot. They will arrest him again for sure if we don't get to him first."

Deklyn rushed from his place, and I followed as soon as I could get my jacket on and stuff Luma in the portable nest.

Out on Goat Square I could see Jasper standing on an up-turned fruit crate, addressing a small crowd that had gathered around him. I hurried closer to hear what he was saying.

"The time for hiding in your homes and shuttered behind storefronts is over! People, all our gold is gone, our dragonka outlawed. I am tired of hiding from these cowards who come in packs like wolves to pick us off. It is time to rise up!" he shouted.

"Easy for you to say!" a poppy dealer I recognized yelled back. "You don't have a home. You don't have a family to feed. You would be just as happy on the streets. But I can't risk my own family."

"Yes, it's true," agreed another.

"It is not so bad these days," a Zsida map merchant said, trying to calm Jasper. "We have food on the table, we continue our studies. So we give a little gold. The dragonka, they were not for us, anyway. These are the worries of the rich."

"That is not true," yelled Jasper. "We—the Blackhearts— have a dragonka. I am not afraid. Let the Boot come and try to take him if they wish. I am not afraid."

"Jasper," Deklyn yelled. "Enough now."

"Enough," he spat contemptuously. "Apparently, it is never enough. You people are asleep."

"You are going to get us arrested!" said Deklyn.

"I want arrest! Instead we are racing dragonka like children at playtime. And you—you let a traitor into our lair," he said, pointing at me.

"Are you accusing me of being in league with the Boot?" Deklyn said, getting up closer to Jasper.

"All cowards are in league with the Boot, like it or not," he said. Deklyn approached him. Jasper looked like he might attack him, then thought the better of it and stepped down from the fruit crate. We watched him stalk off through the crowd, then disappear into the black coffinlike door of the Stone Pillow.

"He has been drinking mead. He can't control himself," said Deklyn.

"The Boot might know about Luma," I said.

"No," said Deklyn. "This is Jozseftown. They protect their own."

LATER THAT EVENING Jasper still had not returned. Deklyn fidgeted on his dragonka chair; then his restlessness got the better of him.

"Come on," he said. "There is a pagan festival over in the Half Not section tonight with a singing dragonka. It should be pretty wild."

"Are you sure we should go out?" I asked.

"Jasper is right about one thing. I am tired of being afraid all the time."

"You are afraid?" I asked, not sure I could believe it.

Deklyn only looked away in what I guessed was shame. My urge to tell him about Luma burned in me stronger than ever, but I could not. I could not trust anybody. And that was *my* shame.

BY THE TIME WE ARRIVED in a deserted apartment building in the Half Not district, the Ceremony of the Maiden Song was about to begin. Except for the time in Archibald's garden, I had never partaken in a dragonka song. Before the crisis, these were highly regulated events, because of the songs' strange and unpredictable effects. Normally, dragonka were taught to sing in chorus: reciting songs that had been passed down through the ages, songs that taught the history of Dravonia through the dreams they conjured. It was only during events like these that dragonka were permitted to sing what came from their hearts. It was considered too unpredictable, and therefore dangerous. But it brought a feeling of solidarity both to the dragonka and the audience, a feeling the children of Jozseftown needed.

Attendants encouraged audience members to sit on the floor: some chose to lie on their backs and gaze up at the sky. After the ambience had been set, a small wagon, pulled on a harness by working dragonka, rode onto the stage. It was festooned with crepe paper, and sparklers blazed along its side; it might have been a Kina wedding-ceremony ship for all its decoration. Once the sparkles burned out, the dragonka that was riding the wagon became visible. It was a stout beast, visibly preening, aware all eyes were on it.

I sat with Luma on my lap, our eyes fixed on the lit-up dragonka who held the floor. Isobel emerged from one of the apartments, her fiddle resting on her shoulder. She came to the center of the circle, and waited for the dragonka to give her the proper signal. With just a flap of its wings the crowd hushed. Silence. It opened its mouth, though a long time seemed to pass before any song came out. (In truth, the sound it made in these moments was inaudible to the human ear, but Luma and the other dragonka heard it, and its voice was fine enough to penetrate the spirit world, where it caused the ghosts that had invaded the courtyard to sway in a melancholy dance and provoked matter that was neither live nor dead to rustle, sending small, almost undetectable sparks off in the air.) But, when the sound did become audible it was like nothing I had ever heard before, neither rough and untamed like the song from the Dragonka Exchange, but dissonant and alluring, like a riddle in musical notation. Isobel began to play along, letting the dragonka song lead her.

And carried in the dragonka song was a charm that set my mind adrift—dreamily floating into a trancelike state as the song filled the room, sudden and fluid, soft and numbing. The notes of the song bounced around in my body, and I gave myself up to them totally. Dreams of past nights appeared before me in the air. Terrible spiders spun neon-colored webs, catching notes in the sticky silk. Then everything froze. That was when the dreams began to spin around my head like a flurry of pictures.

When my head stopped spinning I found myself on an empty street in Jozseftown. But it had changed, somehow. The rambling tenements had been replaced by concrete high-rises with small slits for windows. Factories in the distance belched fog into the air, which hovered over the city like a mourning veil. I began to walk silently. Posters of Archibald were pasted to the walls everywhere; it was almost impossible to cast your gaze in any direction without seeing his likeness. I wandered further into Jozseftown. Up the street I saw a child, walking with his coat collar turned up. I immediately recognized him as Abel. He was older by a few years, and he had lost a lot of weight; the clothing practically fell from his skin. After a few steps Abel paused, looked around furtively, then took a tool from his pocket and went to work scraping Archibald's poster from the wall. Once he got a corner loose, he ripped the poster from its place, then moved on to the next one.

Lost in his work, he failed to notice a group descend upon him. Dressed in military uniforms, emblazoned with gold sun insignias, and led by police dogs, they seemed to have appeared from nowhere. I called out to warn the boy, but my words were soundless: I was an invisible, mute witness to what the dragonka's dream was showing me. I ran to the scene: the patrol had Abel backed against a wall. But as I got closer I realized its dogs weren't police dogs at all: they were a trio of golden dragonka winged and disciplined as trained falcons. The dragonka—with ruby red eyes and claws that shimmered even without sun—appeared to be mechanical versions of the beast I knew. These were nothing like the experiments I had come across before—they had been *perfected*.

The patrol appeared to be enjoying its advantage and taunted the boy. Its voices were suddenly familiar to me. I had not recognized them yet, but when I did I gasped: Sonia and Lenka flanked their commanding officer, Tatiana.

"Look at this worm," said Tatiana.

"Don't you know defacing property is a crime?" said Sonia.

"A crime against us," chimed in Lenka. "The good citizens!"

"Worse," corrected Tatiana. "It is a crime against the people, therefore it is a crime against yourself."

"Worm!" yelled Sonia. Meanwhile the golden dragonka had cornered Abel into a smaller, tighter space, inches from him, their fangs bared and shining with razor sharp teeth. Bright, honey-colored drool spilled from their open mouths.

"Let's take him in," said Lenka. "A little reeducation in the camps down south will do him some good."

"No," said Tatiana. "You can't *re*educate what has never been *educated* in the first place. I have a better idea." She looked around to make sure nobody was watching. "I hate paperwork. It's *sooo* boring. Let's deal with him now. Nobody will know the difference. Who will miss a worm?"

"You mean . . . ?" said Sonia, a mean, greedy glint coming to her eye.

Tatianna nodded, and as though bored, simply let her leash drop. The others followed suit. I turned away when I heard Abel's shriek of agony as the beasts mauled him. The girls crouched down to better watch the bloodshed, encouraging their dragonka with wild, savage shouts.

Suddenly the scene froze as though it was a gory postcard. Then the postcard blew away in the wind, leaving behind only a haze saturated with gold and crimson blood.

"Everybody stand still! Don't move!" somebody from the crowd shouted. It was a human voice, a living voice! The dream was over as suddenly as it had begun. My eyes shot open and there I was, back in that Half Not courtyard. But the scene had changed significantly. In the middle of the floor the singing dragonka was lying on its side, its song cut short by the teeth of a brute Boot wolfhound. A child rushed from the audience to the ailing dragonka. It was Margo! She grabbed the beast as though apprehending it. "Got it, Praise Number One Play Pal!" she yelled. Then it hit me: she was still an agent in the Youth Guard. Other agents began to swarm into the crowd. In the melee I could make out Tatiana, Sonia, and Bianka, all in uniform, directing.

"Grab her!" Tatiana yelled, when she spotted me, though in the mayhem no Boot heard her.

A Boot officer rushed to the middle of the crowd and began to shout orders, which meant that he was not alone. Indeed, looking around, I saw other unknown men encircling the crowd with their batons out.

I realized then that Luma was no longer in my lap. I scanned the courtyard but the dragonka was nowhere to be seen. I began to panic: Luma would not have run off by himself. It wasn't until I looked up that I saw him. Encased in a flurry of gold, he rose into the sky, lifted by a swarm of smaller golden dragonka.

"Luma!" I cried. His head craned toward me, but it was no use. They had him corralled, and were taking him in the direction of the Pava River and the Palace.

Isobel grabbed me. "Unwrap my fazek," she said.

"But Luma!"

"Luma is why I need your help! Undo my fazek!" she repeated calmly. "My wings. Loose them from their harness. Just tear the yarn off. Don't hesitate." I ripped with my fingernails and unraveled the material until Isobel's wings were released from their restraints. She spread them out stiffly, her face creased with pain. She emitted quiet grunts of determination, as though her wings'

freedom hurt more than their binding. I stood back in awe. I had
seen illustrations of winged Half Nots in the books of Pava history, but I had never seen wings as magnificent as this. They spread
out like weathered sails that had been made supple by the winds of
the sea, a translucent parchment held up to the autumn sun.

"Now stand back," Isobel said. She began to flap. At first,
only one wing would move properly, and she fell over in a heap
on the dirt. She stood and began again. Soon her flapping became more coordinated, and she was able to rise a few feet off
the ground before falling back to the earth again. There was a
pause in the commotion as the crowd watched her try to take
awkwardly to the sky. And then it happened: Isobel flew upward,
then flapped after the swarm of golden dragonka. I watched her
fly away, until a hand landed on my shoulder.

"Hurry, let's get out while we can." It was Abel at my side.
"It's a setup. We only have this one chance or we will be arrested."
I stood and followed. Fortunately for us, the rest of the crowd
was not going peacefully either. The Boot had misjudged them
and soon they were overrunning the agents who tried to block the
gate. Fights broke out and I could hear the barking of more red
wolfhounds from the entrance.

Abel and I scampered toward the barking, for there was
no other option. Our only hope of escape was to duck under
the chaos of the rioting. While the Boot officers were busy with
other, more serious threats, Abel was able to dart through a
hole in the crowd and out the door, but when I tried to pass I
felt a hand reach down and grab me by the collar of my coat. I
looked up and saw a bald-headed officer holding me firm. He
pushed me down to the floor, then put his forearm across my
throat. I struggled to break away but his grip was too tight. I
began to choke.

Then suddenly I was free again. Looking up, I saw Jasper
clinging to the back of the agent, like a spider that had dropped
from the ceiling—he was holding a vial under the agent's nose,

causing the man's strength to wane. He looked at me, as if in apology. I gave a quick nod of gratitude and tried to scamper under the legs of the crowd, but at this point the Boot had fully blocked the entrance and were brutally beating all those who made any attempt at escape. Suddenly I heard an ear-piercing shriek come from behind me. And then the room went silent. Everybody turned to look, as if what had happened was unimaginable, even to the most cold-hearted of us.

There, on the floor, was Jasper. Over him stood the Boot officer he had tried to sedate. He was bending over Jasper's unmoving body. The look of pain—or perhaps not pain, more like awakening—on the Boot officer's face was the first thing I registered, then the fact that Jasper had still not moved. I, and everybody else in the room, knew Jasper would not move again, that he was dead, that he had been killed by a blow from the Boot. It was as if when his spirit left his body it had sucked all the energy from the room along with him. Only that it shook me the hardest, because he had died for me, to save me.

Then, a shout broke the silence. The sound pierced my ears like a shattering glass. More surprising, the scream had come from me. I charged the Boot officer, flailing him with my fists. He stood motionless, absorbing my feeble blows. After a moment of this, I was dragged off him from behind by a pair of arms. It was Deklyn, who whispered in my ear: "Come, let's go. We have to get away, now!"

Chapter 20

I was told later that Deklyn led me out of the courtyard with no interference from anybody. I understood that the Boot then resumed their raid, after a troop of reinforcements showed up. Deklyn used a sleeping potion to keep me pacified through the night. I guess caring for me gave him something to do in his mourning.

"Where is Luma?" I said with a start, once I woke.

"Relax," said Deklyn.

"But where is he?"

"Taken by the swarm of golden dragonka," he said. "Isobel has not returned, either."

"And Jasper?" I said. "Was that real, or was that part of my dream?"

"That is real," he said gently.

"Then he is dead?" I asked, though I knew the answer. Deklyn merely nodded. "Where is he now?"

"His body was removed by the Boot. To hide their crime, I suppose." He looked away.

I kept quiet regarding Jasper after that, seeing the look that had passed over Deklyn's face. With Jasper and Isobel gone, there was only me, Abel, and Deklyn. All I wanted was to fall asleep and think about it no more. But Luma was also gone. After all that, the Haints got what they wanted. A full-grown heart for Archibald.

"When I get some messages out to the resistance in other parts of the city, we will be able to better regroup," said Deklyn.

"They are cutting the dragonka up in the basement," I said. "For their hearts. Or, for a heart. Luma's." But I had said it too late.

"What do you mean?" he said.

I explained what I had seen in the Palace. As I did, I could sense thoughts racing behind Deklyn's calm expression.

"Luma is the one, isn't he?" Deklyn finally said.

"Which one?" I asked.

"The one that can save Archibald. The one with Archibald's new heart growing inside him. We heard about it from our spies, but we hear a lot. I thought that was just a silly Half Not rumor."

"No," I said. "It is true. It is why Isobel risked her life to follow them."

"We have to get into the Palace," Deklyn said.

"But how? They already know me by sight there. Besides, you can't just walk straight into the Palace, what with the Boot everywhere."

"We won't," said Deklyn, thinking out loud. "We won't walk straight in. We will walk straight *under*."

"Under? How?"

"With this!" Deklyn said, holding up the map I had given him. "Of course, the Palace has a pneumatic station. All we have to do is follow the tubes, according to the map."

"Let's do it!"

We looked excitedly at each other for a moment.

"We may get Luma, but nothing will bring Jasper back," I said suddenly.

"Nobody said it would," he responded. I fell silent. Deklyn was the most alone person I had ever met.

WE AGREED TO LEAVE that very night. But before we embarked on our mission, we needed a few things, like torches and food. I thought the supplies would be hard to find, now that we were implicated with illegal dragonka racing, but as soon as we left the underground, shopkeepers were beckoning us over, offering us what they had.

"Killing a child, it's not right," one said.

"A child of Jozseftown, moreover," said another.

"Anything you need," said one more, "just come to us. There is a lot of anger here. People have been letting this kind of thing go on too long. And who pays for our complacence? A child."

Abel came up to us. "Didn't you hear? The numbers of the Resistance Movement are swelling. No way the Boot would come back now."

"It is too late for the Resistance Movement," said Deklyn.

"What do you mean? Now we can have as many races as we want."

"You don't understand," said Deklyn. "There is more at work here than just the dragonka races! Grow up a little!" Abel looked stunned. He walked away, hiding his hurt under the brim of his hat.

"You didn't have to do that," I said to Deklyn.

"I know, but he has to learn."

"But you don't have to teach him. Let the world ruin his dreams, if they have to be ruined."

Deklyn looked away. "Come on," he finally said. "We need to get moving. Heaven knows what they are doing with Luma right now."

"He is OK," I said with confidence. "For now." Deklyn nodded, conceding that I could feel things that he could not, regarding Luma. For now, I knew, we were bound by an invisible string.

Later that evening, when we had everything we needed, we departed through the sewer grate. Deklyn unfolded the map and guided the way, but not before he summoned a glow cloud to help us. The sewers under Jozseftown had never felt so spooky yet so familiar to me. I had grown accustomed to dark, forbidden spaces. We started off hesitantly. There could be no making mistakes or getting lost. That might mean certain death, as the sewers were so mazelike. Somewhere under the Pava River, Deklyn hushed me.

"Do you hear that?"

At first I did not know what he was talking about, but after a moment, I heard it, too. The whoosh got loud, then whooshed right past us, like the sound of a stone being thrown past your head. It was the pneumatic system. Somebody was sending mail!

"We have to get moving," he said. "That letter looked like it was heading to the Palace."

"But we are going in the wrong direction," I said. Deklyn had started out down a dark corridor that we had just moments ago passed.

"No," he said. "This is the way."

"You got mixed up," I said. "We were going the other way." But the truth is that the tunnels all looked so alike, even I had become confused.

Indeed, it wasn't long before we realized the layout didn't match with the map. We were lost in the sewers under the Pava River. We bent over the map, studying it.

"I think we are here!" he said, pointing at a coordinate.

"Shhh!" I said. "Do you hear something?"

The sound grew louder. *Feet sloshing through the water.* Lots of feet, like an army of rats were approaching.

"We have to hide!" Deklyn said, looking around.

But there was nowhere to hide, so we fled down the dark tunnel again. But before long came sounds of more rushing feet. Then a glowing appeared from the darkness in front of us. No, they weren't rats, they were tiny golden dragonka, their mouths open, baring their fangs. The discarded, untrainable dragonka that had been so mercilessly cast down the plumbing by the Ministry—grown fierce and bloodthirsty. There was no time, we had to turn and flee in the direction of the other footsteps. Only ahead of us we saw a troop of Boot officers, with a map that looked similar to ours. Their torchlight did not reach us, so for a few moments, we would remain out of view.

Deklyn looked at me and smiled. He put his hand on my shoulder to comfort me. We had tried. Then suddenly I was pulled backward. I toppled through a maintenance shaft and saw Deklyn leap in after me, shutting the gate behind him. I looked up. It was Sytia, the Kubikula.

She hugged me, and I hugged back. Then she beckoned us to follow her, until we arrived at another artery that aligned with the map. She pointed and gestured. We had escaped the Boot once more. Sytia waved goodbye as we continued on our way, her sweet grunts following us as we went. Soon we had crossed under the entire Pava River and headed toward the Palace.

"This must be it," said Deklyn when we arrived. The pipes rose into a tunnel, along which ran a ladder. He took a deep breath, then hoisted himself up. He climbed, then I heard a metallic grinding, a creak, then light poured into the tunnel.

"Come on," he said. And up into the Palace we went.

Chapter 21

Evil is comfortable in silence.

While the city suffered outside, while dragonka were sliced open and children worked in mines, while Jozseftown mourned one of its own, the Palace was quiet. But despite all the time I had spent in the Palace, I was not familiar with its passages and grand rooms, which we slunk through one by one, all unoccupied. Only now and again did we have to hide from servants, though, who moved through the space as though sleepwalking. Then, from the end of the corridor that we had let ourselves into, a noise erupted. It was a howl, like a yell of battle, only more pained. We rushed toward the sound. There I discovered the same door through which Archibald had led me, the one that opened on the stairs to the cellars. We descended, and again the yell sounded. It was Deklyn who held me back when we reached the door from which it came.

We peered around the frame. There was Wormwood, leaning over a table, upon which Archibald the Precious lay.

"It aches," groaned the dictator.

"Hold still," commanded Wormwood. "The heart is winding down. But the time is near when you will need it no longer."

"I don't want this," cried Archibald. "I don't want to be monarch anymore."

"Don't say that!" retorted Wormwood.

"I had a friend, and you sent her away! All I wanted was just one friend."

"You have plenty of friends here with the Haints. They care for you. And soon you will have your very life to thank them for. What could be a better bond of friendship?"

Archibald groaned. "But they don't even know how to play."

"And the Youth Guard. You play with them all the time," said Wormwood.

"They are the worst!" spat Archibald. "The are so mean, and they never play by the rules." Suddenly Archibald's eye caught mine watching him. He gasped.

"My old friend," he said.

"Hush, now," said Wormwood. "You are imagining things again. Just breathe into this cloth. Soon you will have to worry about this faulty heart no more." Wormwood held a cloth up to Archibald's face and the dictator rose in a fit. He fell unconscious. Wormwood laid him flat on the table, then pulled a blanket over his body.

Deklyn and I backed away from the door and crept quietly back down the corridor.

"Can you take us to where the dragonka laboratory is?" Deklyn asked.

"I think so. In fact, I'm pretty sure." Suddenly everything looked familiar. I knew exactly where I was. I quickly guided Deklyn down the corridor, then to the iron door that led to the dragonka laboratory. We opened the great door slowly, then thrust it open when I could see that the room had been emptied. The dragonka were nowhere to be found: the cages had been removed, the beasts cleared from their displays. But beyond the next door were living dragonka, I was sure. I could feel Luma's strange energy. He was alive somewhere.

"Welcome, young visitors," came a voice from behind.

Wormwood strode into the room, followed by a troop of Youth Guard: my former classmates.

"You are so busy with what is ahead of you, you never look behind your own backs," said Tatiana. "We could have tapped you on the shoulder."

"Number One Play Pal finds that noon and midnight are equally observable, though opposite times of the day," said Margo. "If you had learned that, you would have known that which is in front of you, is as it was behind you."

"You have no idea what you are talking about!" I said. "Don't you know that Number One Play Pal is so sick he can't even move? That they are about to implant the heart grown in a dragonka into his body?"

"More dirty Half Not legend," said Sonia.

"It is not," I countered. "Ask Wormwood."

They all turned to their superior. "She is right," said Wormwood. The girls looked at him apprehensively. "Only it is not exactly as she says. It is just that Number One Play Pal has given so much of himself that his heart has simply given out. He is indeed sick. But with everybody's good wishes and help, he will soon return to his full strength. But it is not merely a dragonka heart. It was one fashioned by myself, with materials from the spirit world. It needed a life support system, and dragonka prove an ideal source of nourishment. Indeed, the materials were furnished by Petra K's father. Did you know that, Petra K?"

At that moment I knew he was right: the black caped figure at the bridge who tried to do away with Luma; the fluttering scarf that felt so familiar as it guided me to the laboratory. That was the spirit of my father, trying to guide me, to help me to save Pava from the Haints.

"But he stole the beast when he realized the experiment would be a success. He hid with it in Jozseftown, before trying to kill it, once the dragonka fever broke out. And, as I understand, you saved Luma," said Wormwood. "It is why you are alive right now. We are grateful to you, in our way."

"Where are the dragonka?" shouted Deklyn. "I am here to free them!"

"Ah, yes," retorted Wormwood. "The leader of the Blackhearts is used to making demands. Well, they are here. In this room even. They are everywhere, just look around." With that, he extinguished the lantern. Above us shapes began to form. You could see them emerging and disappearing from an oil-colored circle in the ceiling that looked like a huge water stain. They were the shapes of dragonka, flying round the air above us. Only that they were transparent, like colored mist. The spirits of the murdered dragonka had remained in the Palace. Above them, an enormous swirling cloud spread across the ceiling. No, I realized, it wasn't a cloud at all: it was a hole, and beyond it was the deepest blackness I had ever seen.

"It was an oversight," said Wormwood. "The same ancient sorcery that kept the Haints here, keeps the dragonka spirits as well. We had to get rid of their stuffed bodies, unfortunately. They were too attracted to them, crying all night long, unable to reclaim their living forms. Above them is a gateway to the spirit world, torn open by centuries-old black magic. They should pass through it, but they refuse to depart. Perhaps your spirits too will be trapped here, after we are finished with you. Then you will understand our attachment to this world."

"You can't keep doing their bidding," said Deklyn.

"I can't?" replied Wormwood.

"You don't have to. Let Archibald die, as he should have long ago."

"Why would I do that?" said Wormwood. "When I am one of them?" Before our eyes, Wormwood became translucent. It was true: he was the same as the Haints, whom he was in the service of. "Besides, your efforts—no matter how valiant—are of no use. Luma is being readied for me right now. So I must leave you."

"No!" I cried. But I knew it was true. I began to feel the pull toward sleep, and felt the pastel colors of Luma's dreams begin to infect my sight.

Chapter 22

Wormwood left us to oversee the operation, so it was the troop of Youth Guard who marched us to our holding cells. I kept quiet, stung by their betrayal and use of me. I should have known, even in my days as a Youth Guard, that I would never be one of them. But as we walked, I sensed an unspoken tension arising.

"You didn't tell us that the dragonka were being murdered," I heard Bianka say to Tatiana.

"That is because I didn't know it," she responded.

"Who cares," said Sonia. "It is what the Number One Play Pal wants."

"I care," said Margo. "Or I would have never gone undercover in Jozseftown. The festivals are wonderful. You had a dragonka once, too, Tatiana."

"I know. But be careful what you are saying," said Tatiana.

"Everybody should be careful," said Sonia, not without threat. "It isn't our job to say what is good and right. It is our job to do what we are instructed to do."

"Well, I am tired of playing along," said Bianka, out of nowhere. "I am done here. I don't want to participate in killing dragonka. I *love* dragonka. There, I said it. And Petra K, I'm sorry if I tricked or betrayed you. I always liked you."

Tatiana turned and looked Bianka in the eye, her lips tight with rage. Then she struck her. Bianka appeared stunned, then struck Tatiana back. Sonia and Margo jumped between them, trying to pull one from the other. A glance passed between Deklyn and me, and we both set off running.

"Now look what you've done!" shouted Tatiana. "Go after them!" But her command took some seconds to follow, during which time we were able to disappear behind a closed door, using a chair to prop it closed. But instead of even searching the room, we heard their arguing voices travel past the door.

"Luma!" I said. Soon it would be too late.

"Quiet!" commanded Deklyn. "We can't help him from the dungeons."

"No!" I shouted. I felt a tear in my chest. It was like I was being cut open as well. I went sprawling on the floor. Deklyn knelt down and held me in his arms. The pain was too much for me to keep quiet.

"Go!" I yelled at Deklyn. "Go now! The operation is beginning!" He looked torn, his face tight with fret. He bent over and kissed my forehead. I could just see the top of the black heart poking from the top of his blouse. I concentrated on the image—holding the broken black heart there in my mind—to try to calm myself, to keep it in my head and push the pain out. By the time I opened my eyes, Deklyn had removed the chair from the door and had fled the room. I let my head fall back, and cried out in pain. It was too much. I took the dragonka voice machine from my pocket and cranked the handle. The soft song lulled me. Soon, I was asleep.

In a place in my dreams the dragonka song found me. A figure appeared to me momentarily, its form transparent, like the outline of a body emerging from the fog.

"I cannot stay long," the shape said. I could see that his outline was vague, blending into the wall behind him. "The spirit world has a claim on me, and it is difficult to hold my form."

"Father?" I said, startled by my sudden realization. I started to get up, but he halted me with a wave of his ghostly hand.

"It will do no good," he laughed. "Your touch would go right through me."

"There is so much I want to ask," I said.

"We don't have time now," he replied.

"But . . . what happened to you . . . Mother said—"

"Petra K, listen to me," said Jozsef K. "I want to talk to you and tell you everything that happened. My life was complicated, and ended too soon."

"Ended?"

"Like I said, I live in the spirit world, Petra K."

"But you are here now," I said. "Are you one of them? Do you work for the spirits?"

"I did. I had no choice. There is a gateway in the Palace to the spirit world. I steal in, I steal out. I *steal*. The Haints needed help in attaining materials for their experiments, so I helped. I am not proud. But I quit when I discovered their real purpose."

"You tried to drown Luma," I said. "How could you do that? You don't go deserting helpless things to their fates. It's not fair!"

"I can't explain it all," he said. "Besides, you saved him. Now the entire responsibility is on your shoulders."

Then my father began to fade. He waved his arms around in front of himself like a blind man.

"Are you there? Are you there Petra K?"

"Yes, Father," I said.

"I am sorry, Petra K."

"Goodbye," he said. "I am fading, for good right now. But if you play the dragonka song, you will be able to call my presence, if not in shape, then in feeling."

"Goodbye," I said, and then he was once again lost to me.

When I woke, I was alone. The door was wide open, and the pain had disappeared from my chest. I ran my finger along the spot where the attack had been, but felt nothing except smooth skin. It was as though the cut had healed. Luma was safe, I could feel it: I still felt his presence. Deklyn had succeeded.

I heard footsteps coming from the other end of the hall-way, approaching. It would be Deklyn, I was sure, come to retrieve me. We would return to Jozseftown, and I would go home, to where I belonged, with the dragonka free from harm. We would have festivals, and I would invite the Blackhearts to live with us in the spare rooms of our house. We would live happily.

A child's shape crossed into the doorway. Archibald appeared neither young nor old, but ageless, his face looking like a shrunken apple. He was beatific. Now that he had the heart of a dragonka, the heart of Luma.

"Are you well?" he asked.

"I should ask you the same thing," I said bitterly.

"The Haints are waiting in the ballroom. We are going to have a celebration. Every child in the Youth Guard had a birthday, and now it is my turn. We did not want to start without you."

I ignored the invitation. "So all this dragonka fever, all the quarantine was about finding the dragonka that was growing your heart?"

"It was the Haints' doing. It is what they have worked on for so long. For longer than either of us have been alive. But look! We are both alive now! Let us go and celebrate. You can live here with me. I already asked the Haints. They say it is OK. They are not mad at you at all. In fact, Wormwood is quite fond of you."

"I would never live here with you," I said levelly, but not as cruelly as I had hoped. I could feel that the attraction to Luma now had me confused about Archibald. He was so familiar in his presence, with Luma's heart.

"Don't say that. I feel that you could do good in the Palace affairs. You could have a whole muse of golden dragonka to yourself. As many as you want. You wouldn't even have to care for them, it would all be done for you."

"Where is Deklyn?" I said.

"Your other friend?" he asked, and not without jealousy.

"My *only* friend," I said.

Archibald looked stung. "He and his organization are still a threat, or so say the Haints. He is going to be sent to the mines. It is out of my control."

"So, you say you are a human now?"

"Yes," he stated calmly.

"Without a mechanical heart?"

"Yes."

"Then I will make you a deal," I said.

"Tell me," he said.

"I'll stay if you can do one thing."

"What?"

I took an empty potion vial from my pocket. "Fill it with tears. Pay me in tears, and then we're even." Archibald looked at me with surprise. I closed my eyes. I waited as Archibald held the vial in front of himself.

"It's no use . . . " he said.

"Then just one tear," I said.

"I can't," he said, handing the vial back.

"Then let Deklyn and the other Blackhearts go, let the dragonka live free, and I will stay."

Archibald looked touched, as though he actually might cry. I felt nothing but pity for him, my brother in spirit.

"It shall be done. . . ." he said.

"It shall not," came a voice from behind Archibald. It was Wormwood, who had been listening outside the door. He entered the room. He was wearing a black dinner jacket, ready for the celebration of Archibald's perpetual reign.

"Come now," he said. "The Ministry of Unlikely Occurrences is expecting the both of you. Petra K, you will find your dress in the wardrobe."

Archibald smiled at me. It was clear he was used to being directed by the Haints; that his own will had dissolved under the direction of theirs. But somewhere inside him was a piece of Luma, and I still had control over that part. I could tell by the way he could not take his eyes off me, as though looking for my approval.

"Very well," I said. "I will put on the dress and join you. But you must not leave my side all night."

"Absolutely," he stated, eyes entranced with me. "And you will stay with me in the Palace. I shall learn to cry. For you."

"Yes," I said. "*Yes you will.*"

I CHANGED WHILE Archibald waited outside the room. Now that I had his confidence, I was going to use it to its fullest. At the very least, I would be able to kill him, even if it meant risking my own life. I owed Luma, Deklyn, and Jozseftown that much. After I had dressed, Archibald escorted me to the ballroom in the cellar, where the Haints were already comfortably into their celebration. The room was spectacularly changed from when I was last there. Crepe-paper depictions of the Haints festooned the walls; alchemists and charlatans alike were mixing with each other. Sonia was there, but the other girls were absent. Moreover, leaders from the Zsida and Half Not community were present, as were members of Pava society; even a few members of the Stink Clovers. The Palace doors had been thrown open, now that the Haints had nothing to fear. It was like everybody had just given up. The spirits of murdered dragonka floated harmlessly above.

"Come on," he said, tugging me into the room by my hand, toward the Haints. "May I present you to Jacob of Mangolia?" said Archibald. I recognized him as the general I had met earlier. "There was a time when he could weave yarn into gold."

"Hello," I said as politely as I could. An elegantly dressed man glided across the ballroom. "And Nester Nessesarian," said the dictator. Nester had formerly been on the chariot. "Inventor of the fire stone, still available at certain Zsida shops." Another Haint drifted over. And so it happened, one after the other was introduced to me. Some even apologized for the way I was treated. Forthrightly, a ghastly looking string band struck up a waltz. The Haints began to dance, twirling each other around expertly.

"They dance well," I said to Archibald.

"They are not bad spirits," he said. "They are not evil, not like you think. It is just that they want to stay here, in this world. In this palace. Who wouldn't, after all?"

We watched from the side of the room. The Haints poured mead and amber-sweet wine down their gullets. They flew under tables and around chairs, chasing anybody who showed fear. They were repulsive, and the room reeked with the smell of their living death. I did my best to stay still, as Archibald had instructed.

"Aren't they wonderful?" Archibald said.

"Oh yes, they are super," I lied.

"Come, let's dance," he said.

"So, if you had died, the Haints would have withered away."

"Eventually, yes. Or they would have been cast out of the Palace. I saved them, you see. And they saved me. You can see how happy they have been made."

Archibald took me by the waist and swayed awkwardly to the music. I looked at him: he appeared transcendent.

"I want you to try something with me," I said. "It's a game we can play."

"Oh good. I love playing with you."

"Breathe at the same rate as me," I said.

"Like this?" he asked, synchronizing his breathing with mine.

If it was true that Isobel could meld with Luma's heart, then I could do the same with Archibald. It was the same heart. And, indeed, as we breathed together I could feel the spirit breaching begin, and Archibald's will succumbing to mine. Nobody noticed what was happening, but I had Archibald under my control. I could do anything. I could stop that stolen heart from beating. And that is exactly what I did. He inhaled deeply and clutched at his chest. Only a few more moments now . . .

But then I was suddenly caught by the look in his eyes. It was innocent. He did not deserve to die. There would have to be another way. I took a final deep breath and released him from the spirit breach.

He looked at me sharply, as though I had slapped him.

"I don't like that game," he said.

"It's not nice to control people," I said. "The way you control the kids in the Youth Guard, the way you send people to the mines, the way you control the fate of the dragonka."

"I don't like how you are talking, either."

"Too bad," I said. He dropped my hands in frustration. Now, the Haints were beginning to notice the rift. They flew closer, to protect Archibald if needed.

"I don't want to play with you anymore," he said. He began to whimper, then tightened his face to control himself. "You won't have a single tear, Petra K! That is the last thing you will get from me! Take her away from me!"

At his command the Haints dove at me. I was defenseless against their overpowering fury. They swallowed me up as though I was caught in a tornado. I rose from the ground, the haunted, ghastly faces swirling around me.

"Stop," somebody yelled. It was Wormwood. Only he was not facing us; he was facing the balcony that looked out over the city. "They are coming!" he said.

"Who?" asked Archibald.

"Look!" he said. The Haints suddenly lost interest in me, letting me fall to the floor with a thud. I gathered myself and hobbled to an unoccupied window to see what was happening. Outside the Palace walls, a mighty crowd of people had amassed. It looked like some sort of riot, as though the entire city had gone mad. Some were carrying torches, many were armed. The JRM must have brought the people together. Huge banners flew, with broken black hearts painted across them. Moreover, men in the freezing winter air had ripped their shirts from their bodies, revealing black hearts they had etched onto their chests with coal. I saw more than one Boot poster adulterated, with Jasper's likeness superimposed over that of Archibald. There was an army of Blackhearts outside, because of Jasper's courageous death. They were coming to overtake the Palace.

"Where is the Boot Guard?" shouted Wormwood.

"Overrun," came a voice from the chamber door. It was Bianka, only now she had changed from her Youth Guard uniform into street clothing. "Overrun, or they switched sides and joined the resistance. Just like me."

"This is impossible," shrieked Wormwood. "It is tyranny. It is treason."

"No. It is none of those things. It is justice," came another voice. I recognized it immediately. It was Deklyn. He had escaped, and behind him were Tatiana and Margo, who had also shed their uniforms in favor of street clothing. Plus, to my relief, Isobel hovered above him, her wings radiant in the paraffin light.

I looked to see where Archibald was, but the Haints had surrounded him, protecting him.

"Raise the battlements," said Wormwood. "Let loose all the wolfhounds and the golden dragonka, whether they are battle-ready or not. Let's see how strong their resolve is." Boot faithful rushed off to do his bidding. Great shutters closed over the windows, blocking everybody inside from the battle that ensued. Once the room was sealed, a strange calm fell, as though we were all waiting out a storm. It was noiseless, but for the pathetic sound of Archibald's renewed whimpering. I took his hand in a moment of compassion, but he only pulled it away from me. I sighed, then returned to the ballroom.

THE REVOLUTION HAD INFILTRATED THE PALACE, and the people of Pava were rising up against the Haints. But all was not won. Once I entered the ballroom, I saw Wormwood directing the Haints in a last attack on the living.

"You may win the battle outside, but what is important is in here. And, as you know, you cannot kill what is already dead. You, on the other hand, will die quite easily," Wormwood said to one and all.

Then the Haints turned their fury on Deklyn and my former classmates. They were plucked from the ground and carried in the air. Deklyn and Bianka were tossed to-and-fro across the arched ceiling, like birdies in a game of badminton. The Blackheart leader, for all his bravery, was no match for centuries of brooding evil. But in the midst of that mayhem, something curious happened. The dragonka spirits began to nip at the Haints with their jaws. First, they did so tentatively, as if to test their reaction, then they acted with more force. Soon, there was a flurry of dragonka attacking each Haint, with only more coming through the portal. All of the Haints got involved, leaving Archibald alone. He crouched in the corner, shivering.

The city had to be banished of the Haints for good. But, unfortunately, the dragonka were no match for the fury of the dark spirits, whose time in the world had nourished them with an agility that was near human.

But the battle was not over. As the hole into the spirit world became more porous, other creatures began seeping through: first a school of seahorses bobbed in the air. Then a griffin emerged, decided it didn't like what it saw, and disappeared again. A white, ghostly elephant also made an appearance, then charged off through the palace wall and into the Pava night sky. This gave the

Haints no pause. Soon they had chased the very last of the drag-onka through the hole, back into the spirit world.

When they were finished, they returned to the ballroom floor. Jacob of Mangolia—the fat general—drew his sword, and held it high.

"Long live Archibald!" he bellowed.

"Long live Archibald!" the other Haints repeated.

He pointed the tip of his sword at me. "Hail Archibald, or lose your head."

"That is not necessary," said Archibald.

"Nobody will stand in our way, now. Pava will gratify our goldlust for centuries. We will bleed you of the stuff."

"But I am the leader," said Archibald, as if somebody had broken the rules of a card game.

"Wormwood, silence the child," said Nester. Wormwood put his arm over Archibald's mouth, and kept it there despite how the boy squirmed.

"Now," he said to Deklyn and me, "Hail."

"Never," I said. "All hail the Blackhearts and Jozseftown. Hail Jasper, whom you murdered. Jasper," I called. "Jasper!" I do not know if he actually would have cut my head off. I never had to find out, because from the hole came a rumbling. As it grew louder, it began to shake the ceiling, and bits of plaster rained down on us. Every last being—living and spirit—cocked its head upward. Then, through the hole, taking out a good portion of the ceiling with it, burst the spirit of the ancient Pava dragon—Ruki Mur—and on its back was Jasper. The progenitor of every living dragonka had returned to Pava, and it too had revenge on its mind.

Chapter 23

If anybody wants to know if Haints bleed, I have the answer. They do not, though a light green mist escapes where their plasma has been torn. Ruki Mur ripped through them like hungry teeth through boiled cabbage leaves. It was not pretty. Jasper, or, the spirit of Jasper, rode expertly the back of the beast. His black heart tattoo was still visible; it had followed him to the spirit world. Smaller dragonka, too, came to get in their licks, tearing what remained of the Haints to tattered shreds. I think I was the only one who noticed, but Wormwood slipped into the portal uninjured.

As terrible things were happening above, Archibald also stole away. One moment he was there, and the next he had disappeared behind a tapestry. I raced after and found that there was a hidden door that opened onto a spiraling case of stairs. I rushed in pursuit; he could run, but I already knew all of Archibald's favorite hiding places. Of course, I should not have gone, or I should have at least brought somebody with me, but there was no time for that kind of thinking. Archibald had to be delivered to his fate, for the city's sake, and for the sake of Luma.

The passageway led to the dungeons. There I was pretty sure I knew what direction he would take. I raced to Archibald's playroom. From there, he would try to escape from the hatch that held Archibald's pet dragonka. I burst into the room, and was immediately brought up short by what I saw. The dragonka had been loosed from their pens and were running around the grounds. There stood Abel, holding Archibald by the neck. Other members of the JRM were there too. Many different faces from Jozseftown cheered or looked on. Isobel played her violin wildly, controlling the berserking hoard of dragonka.

"I'm going to be the one to do it!" Abel yelled. "I'm going to be the one to put to death this menace. I'm all grown up now!" he shouted to anybody within earshot. He raised a dagger high.

"No!" I yelled. He paused, arm still raised, and looked at me.

"He has Luma's heart," I said. "Can't you feel it?"

"You don't feel those things when you are grown up," he said.

"Yes," I said. "You do. Don't let that part die."

Abel looked down at Archibald. I could tell he felt the presence of Luma's heart. The question was, did he care? Suddenly, I saw a tear form in Archibald's eye. It was one of Luma's tears, long and silvery.

"Look at his chest," I said. Abel dropped his dagger, then opened Archibald's shirt, revealing a deep carmine scar around his heart, blackened, like Abel's own. Abel gasped.

"He was an innocent. Just like us."

Abel nodded. He began to weep himself, then released the ousted dictator.

I escorted Archibald back into the Palace. I took him to the room he had let me sleep in, and found a stuffed toy to put him to bed with. The tears, once begun, sprung without ceasing.

"Stay here," I said. Archibald cried, and within moments he was asleep.

MEANWHILE, THE PEOPLE OF THE CITY had overtaken the Palace. Doors were broken down, and the looting of the treasures became an ugly sight. But aside from that, it was a night for celebration. First, the prisoners in the cages that hung on the road to the Palace were released, then bonfires were built around the grounds, and musicians—Half Not, Zsida, and Pavaian alike— were called to play. And play they did, into the early dawn, as whole sides of ox and mutton from the Palace's own rations were turned over spits. There was a turkey stuffed with a pheasant, which was in turn stuffed with pigeon, all roasted over the coals. Potatoes where chopped up with red-hot paprika and doused with sunflower oil, then fried. Honey and poppy pastries were unwrapped from wax paper, and logs of cherry strudel were passed out for dessert. Everybody sipped mead and soon became dizzy and brazen on its effect. It was luxuriant and decadent, a feast fit for victory.

I was drunk on the food. I sat against an old chair and watched men and boys take turns jumping over the dying fire. Soon somebody broke out a hurdy gurdy, and another dragged out a half-broken cimbalom, a dulcimerlike instrument played like a piano but with tiny hammers hitting its strings. Deklyn produced a mandolin, and the sound of traditional Dravonian music filled the air: ancient song that rhapsodized the country's founding, the trials of the tribes that had settled the land. Then they sang centuries-old drinking songs. The music infected me, and before I knew it I was dancing around the fire. One boy was my partner, then another, before I found Deklyn twirling me around in circles before we collapsed onto the dirt.

"You should get some sleep," he said.

"No way," I said. "I'm going to enjoy this while it lasts."

"We couldn't have done this without you, you know."

I looked away from his gaze. It was too intense, like he wanted to possess my spirit, the way he so easily possessed anything else he wanted.

THE PARTY LASTED EARLY INTO THE DAY. The doors to the Palace had been thrown open and dragonka raced up and down the hallways. The mess they made was precocious and wonderful. They had luxury in their blood, and once they got a taste of it, they smothered themselves in its fat, rolling in Archibald's bed sheets, napping in the crystal chandeliers, tearing smoked meat from the hooks in the kitchen and gobbling rare and expensive truffles as though they were popcorn. The spirit of Ruki Mur wrested herself from the Palace walls and flew above the city, wings spread, hovering like a zeppelin for their amusement, the tiny dragonka swirling around her, paying homage, chasing each other under her ghostly protection. Floating in the air they looked like bees swarming around a hive or like cherubim around a cloud.

And so they played through the day and into the next night as well. It felt to the people of Pava like freedom had been so unbearably long in arriving. They simply could not contain themselves. Great races took place throughout the Palace and in the Imperial gardens. Then, as the beasts mellowed, Isobel gathered the dragonka together for a song. Their voices rose over Pava, infecting the dreams of the city's children; for a dragonka song can strengthen one's imagination, and this song roused them to fantastic heights. The children of Pava experienced a collective dream that night, and would be surprised in the morning when they compared their dreams. It was a beautiful, original song and all the Blackhearts felt content for its duration, as though good-natured spirits were in their midst, clapping through the clatter of the ivy that swayed in the wind. As though the night sky was brightened with the song.

But there was still an emptiness inside of me, one I felt might never be relieved. I made my way past children sleeping in the grand Palace corridors, even stepping gingerly over a few Kubikula who had come above ground to join the celebration. The ballroom was empty now. The dragonka spirits had departed, and the rest of the JRM were outside. I got down on the floor and lay on my back, staring at the hole in the ceiling. I felt like the room began to move, but no—it was the hole that began to swirl. It was closing, like a wound healing itself. I knew Luma was there, frolicking in the spirit world, with his heart very much alive in this one, giving life to a good person. The hole closed and sealed itself, disappearing into the ceiling as though it had never been there at all. It left me with this thought: *The universe is empty, but it is full with what we give to it.*

"Petra K," came a voice. It was Archibald. He was dressed and had obviously been up for a while already. "I have just come from a meeting with the elders of the Zsida, Half Not, and Pavain communities. The Ministry of Unlikely Occurrences has been officially disbanded."

"But who will lead Pava?" I asked.

"Me," he said. "I am still monarch, aren't I?" he said.

"Yes," I said.

"Only that now I will only take council with the wisest leaders from across the county."

"I am glad," I said.

"I have something for you," he said. From his tunic he produced an orb that glowed dimly in the twilight.

"What is it?" I asked.

"I insisted that the dragonka that nurtured my heart be kept alive in some fashion. This is the spirit of Luma, encased in crystal. Hold it." I took the orb from him. Indeed, the ball was warm and radiated Luma's unique charm. I held it close to me.

"I have had enough of spirits around me. And Luma belongs to you. Thank you, Petra K," he said, then disappeared into the Palace.

FOR THE FIRST TIME IN SO LONG, I thought of my mother. With the Palace waking up, I departed, walking past the charred remains of the battle. On the Palace lawn I saw pieces of the golden dragonka strewn about, and Half Not beggars come to reclaim the precious metal from their lifeless bodies. A final golden kiš-dragonka—the lone survivor of the battle—flew at me, buzzing around my face. I swatted at it and watched it fly dizzily away. Farther on, I saw that the propaganda posters of Archibald had been set on fire, ash from the burned paper used to etch black hearts on the wall.

I CROSSED THE KARLOW BRIDGE, the statues of the city's founders and saints looking over me, as though appraising my steps. And, finally, into Jozseftown I strode. The markets, on this early morning, were open, as though nothing had happened. I walked unnoticed through Goat Square and down my street, to our ivy-covered townhouse. Up I went, not through the door, but scaling the latticework to my window.

I had come home, but there was no home anymore. I crept past my mother's door, and took the stairs two at a time to my attic bedroom. There, I slept for what felt like days, though it was only overnight. When I woke again, I looked out my window, over the city. An automaton walked stiffly down the street; an errant goat clopped loudly on the cobblestones. Somebody was reopening the marionette shop across the street. It was my neighborhood. Wistfully, I took a fountain pen from my desk and dipped it in black ink. I carefully drew a heart over my chest. At that moment, I knew my home was not my home anymore. I packed a small bag, keeping Luma's orb in my pocket, and headed down the steps.

I paused by my mother's door, then quietly pushed it open. I walked to her bed, hearing her breathing come heavy in a restless, fitful sleep. On the night table I saw a pot of tepid tea. From my pocket, I took the wind-up dragonka song box. I cranked the handle and let it play a little. My mother's face became placid, and, I believe, content. I placed it by the bed. After that, I left the house, for good this time.

I stopped by the broken fish fountain. The crowds had returned to Jozseftown again; the market stalls were all open and filled with wares. It was almost as if nothing had changed.

Hesitantly, from the crowd, an old woman fixed her eyes on me, then hobbled in my direction. She was dressed in fine silk material, with a peacock feather that extended from her hat, and looked like she might have come from the Palace district.

"I want to thank you. It is Pivo. I got him back. I was just sitting there, eating a bowl of kasha, and through the window flew my Pivo, my only companion in my old age."

"Your drangonka?"

"Yes. My neighbor had turned him in to the Boot. I was sure he was dead. Thank you."

"Ma'am, I am not a Blackheart."

"This is no time to be coy. They told me to look for the black heart," the old woman said, glancing down at my open collar. I realized the mistake, the inky black heart I had traced.

"I'm not . . ." I began to protest again, but was interrupted by a voice behind me.

"It was the people of Jozseftown. You have them to thank." It was Deklyn.

"Then thank them for me," she said, hobbling away, back to her own home and her dragonka.

"Do you think that you are entitled to be a Blackheart?" Deklyn asked.

I shook my head while I put my hand to my chest, covering the place where the heart would be, as though taking an oath of innocence.

"I saw that messy stain you drew on yourself. No need to hide it," he said.

My face reddened, and I turned away from him. I felt shamed, like I had been caught playing a private pantomime in front of the mirror. I looked shyly over my shoulder: he was still there, considering me.

"Come on," he said. "Come with me."

I WAS WELCOMED INTO THE BLACKHEARTS' OLD LAIR by Abel, and Liverpool, a dragonka he had acquired from the Palace.

"I am ready," I said.

Deklyn smiled.

The others crowded around. Deklyn sterilized a needle over a paraffin lamp and dipped it into a bottle of black ink. I undid the top buttons of my shirt and steeled myself by biting down on a cinnamon stick.

"With this mark you will never have to worry about being alone, you will always have somebody to watch out for you. You will always have a family. So it is with one of us, so it is with all of us," Deklyn said. The other Blackhearts cheered their approval, patting me on the back. Abel leaned over to kiss me on the cheek. Rufus frolicked in his pen, and the spirit of Luma glowed a bright purple in its orb. The tattoo—the black heart with a jagged break down the center, broken like their city was broken by the great Pava River, like their families were broken—would make me one of them. I closed my eyes as Deklyn pressed the needle into my breast, breaking the skin with its black potion, forever marking me as Petra Blackheart.

Also Available

Voyage to Kazohinia. A rediscovered classic of dystopian fiction
"Massively entertaining." —Gregory Maguire, author of *Wicked*
978-0-9825781-2-4

Ballpoint: *A Tale of Genius and Grit, Perilous Times, and the Invention
that Changed the Way We Write*
978-0-9825781-1-7

Eastern Europe!: *Everything You Need to Know About the History
(and More) of a Region that Shaped Our World and Still Does*
978-0-9850623-2-3

The Essential Guide to Being Hungarian: *50 Facts & Facets of
Nationhood*
978-0-9825781-0-0

The Essential Guide to Being Polish: *50 Facts & Facets of Nationhood*
978-0-9850623-0-9

Illegal Liaisons. "A merciless comedy of modern manners and
the politics of desire." —*Publishers Weekly*
978-0-9850623-6-1

Just a Bite: *A Transylvania Vampire Expert's Short History of the Undead*
978-0-9825781-4-8

New Europe Books
Williamstown, Massachusetts

New Europe Books

Find our titles wherever books are sold,
or visit www.NewEuropeBooks.com for order information.

ABOUT THE AUTHOR

M. Henderson Ellis is the author of *Keeping Bedlam at Bay in the Prague Café* (New Europe Books, 2012) and the founding editor of one of Eastern Europe's most distinguished English-language literary magazines, *Pilvax*. A Chicago native and graduate of Bennington College, Ellis has lived for the past decade in Budapest, Hungary, and lived previously in Prague.

PRAISE FOR THE AUTHOR'S PREVIOUS BOOK

"[G]enuine imagination and an energetic wit."
—*Publishers Weekly*

"[A] manic, wild ride."
—*Booklist*

"A hilarious hallucinatory satire, built on shots of caffeine."
—**Amanda Stern,** author of *The Long Haul*